"Okay, You Win,"
Amelia Said Breathlessly.

Tyler nearly forgot to breathe.

"I win?"

Amelia glared. "You know what I mean! Don't play coy with me at this late date, mister." She leaned forward to make her point.

He stood up. Their faces were mere inches apart, their breath caressing each other's cheeks.

"When?" he asked.

"The sooner, the better. Then maybe you'll get this out of your system and I can get back to work."

Tyler's voice stopped her cold. "I have a small problem. I don't know your last name...or where you live."

Oh, God! "Umm...it's Champion. And don't bother picking me up. Just meet me here around nine." She hesitated, then went on. "It's that or nothing. I have two jobs. It's impossible to come earlier."

"I'll take it," he said softly.

And I'll take you. Anywhere...on any terms.

Dear Reader,

In honor of International Women's Day, March 8, celebrate romance, love and the accomplishments of women all over the world by reading six passionate, powerful and provocative new titles from Silhouette Desire.

New York Times bestselling author Sharon Sala leads the Desire lineup with *Amber by Night* (#1495). A shy librarian uses her alter ego to win her lover's heart in a sizzling love story by this beloved MIRA and Intimate Moments author. Next, a pretend affair turns to true passion when a Barone heroine takes on the competition, in *Sleeping with Her Rival* (#1496) by Sheri WhiteFeather, the third title of the compelling DYNASTIES: THE BARONES saga.

A single mom shares a heated kiss with a stranger on New Year's Eve and soon after reencounters him at work, in *Renegade Millionaire* (1497) by Kristi Gold. *Mail-Order Prince in Her Bed* (#1498) by Kathryn Jensen features an Italian nobleman who teaches an American ingenue the language of love, while a city girl and a rancher get together with the help of her elderly aunt, in *The Cowboy Claims His Lady* (#1499) by Meagan McKinney, the latest MATCHED IN MONTANA title. And a contractor searching for his secret son finds love in the arms of the boy's adoptive mother, in *Tangled Sheets, Tangled Lies* (#1500) by brand-new author Julie Hogan, debuting in the Desire line.

Delight in all six of these sexy Silhouette Desire titles this month…and every month.

Enjoy!

Joan Marlow Golan

Joan Marlow Golan
Senior Editor, Silhouette Desire

Please address questions and book requests to:
Silhouette Reader Service
U.S.: 3010 Walden Ave., P.O. Box 1325, Buffalo, NY 14269
Canadian: P.O. Box 609, Fort Erie, Ont. L2A 5X3

SHARON SALA

Amber by Night

Published by Silhouette Books

America's Publisher of Contemporary Romance

SILHOUETTE BOOKS

ISBN 0-373-76495-2

AMBER BY NIGHT

Copyright © 2003 by Sharon Sala

This edition published by arrangement with Harlequin Books S.A.

Visit Silhouette at www.eHarlequin.com

Printed in U.S.A.

Books by Sharon Sala

Silhouette Desire

Amber by Night #1495

Silhouette Intimate Moments

Annie and the Outlaw #597
The Miracle Man #650
When You Call My Name #687
Shades of a Desperado #757
*Ryder's Wife #817
*Roman's Heart #859
*Royal's Child #913
A Place To Call Home #973
Mission: Irresistible #1016
Familiar Stranger #1082
The Way to Yesterday #1171

*The Justice Way

Silhouette Books

36 Hours
For Her Eyes Only

3, 2, 1...Married!
"Miracle Bride"

Going to the Chapel
"It Happened One Night"

SHARON SALA

is a child of the country. As a farmer's daughter, she
found her vivid imagination made solitude a thing to
cherish. During her adult life, she learned to survive by
taking things one day at a time. An inveterate dreamer,
she yearned to share the stories her imagination created.
For Sharon, her dreams have come true, and she claims
one of her greatest joys is when her stories become tools
for healing.

Chris and Mabel Shero were my maternal grandparents, but all of their grandchildren called them Grampy and Grand. They were two of the kindest and most caring people I ever knew, and they adored each other. Every time I think of soul mates, I think of them.

Grand was always full of quotes and sayings, so besides teaching me how to bake bread, she was constantly filling my head with things she thought I needed to know. One of the earliest homilies that I can remember was her quoting, "Oh what a tangled web we weave when first we practice to deceive." Of course I wanted an explanation, and in her most forthright manner, she pared that down to fit my limited vocabulary by telling me that lies grow faster than weeds and are harder to get rid of. Since one of my chores was weeding our vegetable garden, I immediately understood.

So, because this story starts with the telling of a lie, I thought it fitting to give credit to two of the people who taught me the meaning of truth.

To Christopher and Mabel Shero.
Always my touchstones.
Forever my loves.

One

The back alley between Fourth Street and Beauregard Boulevard was not the best place in Tulip, Georgia to break down, but worn u-joints were not a model of consideration. And, considering the fact that it was nearly sundown and the only thing stirring in Tulip at this time of evening was air, Tyler Savage was in a bit of a fix.

He lay flat on his back beneath his pickup truck, cursing the fading light and his bad luck all in the same disgusted breath. And, because he was so focused on finding and stopping the flow of oil dripping from somewhere up above his head, he didn't hear the sound of running footsteps coming down the alley until they were almost upon him.

Instinctively, he turned to look and got a fairly good view of a woman running down the alley. From where he was lying, he couldn't see much above her neck, but he got a real good look at the gray sweatsuit she was wearing. It was nondescript, but that was where ordinary ended. She had exceedingly long legs, a trim figure and a bosom that was bouncing enticingly as she ran.

Out of appreciation…and partly out of habit…he whistled and then grinned when she broke her stride. But before he could drag himself out from beneath the truck and procure an introduction, a large dollop of oil took the opportunity to fall. It landed directly on the bridge of Tyler's nose before splattering equally in both directions and blinding him to everything but the quick sting of oil filming across his vision.

"Son of a…"

He grabbed for a rag, but not in time to stop the damage. With another muttered curse, he came out from under the truck, wiping at his eyes with the rag and both hands. By the time he could see, she was nowhere in sight. In disgust, he kicked a rear tire with the toe of his boot and started walking in the direction of Raymond Earl Showalter's house. Raymond Earl owned the only garage in town and, in his single days, had been a good running buddy of Tyler's.

As Tyler walked, he kept trying to think who in the world that woman could have been. To his knowledge, none of the females in Tulip were much prone to physical fitness to prolong their youthful appearances. They seemed more inclined to the old southern way of life of getting married while they were still in the bud. It was only after several years of wedded bliss and all the babies they intended to bear, that a goodly portion of them saw it as their just due to bloom to full figure. And to the ladies' credit, none of the husbands Tyler knew seemed upset with the deal.

So, if he hadn't imagined what he'd just seen, and he was pretty sure he hadn't lost his instincts for the opposite sex, there was a new girl in town. But who in the world was she?

While Tyler was eliciting Raymond Earl's aid, Amelia Beauchamp was hunkered down in the front seat of Rae-

lene Stringer's old car and praying for all she was worth
as Raelene sped out of town.

The near-confrontation in the alley had been a close call,
Amelia's first since starting her charade. The fact that
she'd almost been caught wasn't nearly as frightening as
who'd nearly caught her.

Tyler Savage, of all people! Her heart was still pounding
as she finally straightened up in the seat and began putting
on her makeup and fixing her hair. She yanked down the
sun visor and then grimaced. You sissy, she thought, and
then relaxed as her hands flew about a task that was now
familiar. The fact that her heart was racing and her eyes
were glitter bright was entirely due to that man. Tyler Dean
Savage was Tulip's resident rake. That he was also single
and constantly on the make did nothing to help her equi-
librium.

Amelia had had a *thing* for Tyler Savage for more years
than she cared to remember. Unfortunately, Tyler wouldn't
have given Amelia the time of day. She glared at herself
in the mirror and sighed. But Amber…that was another
story. If only, she thought, she dared be one and the same.

The grandfather clock standing guard in the darkened
hallway struck an accusing two o'clock, in the morning,
that is—as Amelia Beauchamp crept back into the house
where she lived, shut and locked the front door and then
breathed a quiet sigh of relief.

Another night of secrets was behind her, and with only
six hours of promised sleep beckoning her to her bed, she
slipped quietly up the staircase and into her room, taking
care not to step on the third step from the top. It squeaked.

The beautiful face staring back at her in the mirror over
her dresser would have shocked her aunts. They would not
have recognized their Amelia. She leaned forward, frowning at her reflection as she slipped dangling ruby earrings
from her ears. With weariness in every movement, she

brushed her rich, brown hair into a smooth, orderly fashion and coiled it into one long loose braid. Jabbing her finger into a jar of cold cream, she swiped the thick lotion roughly across her mouth and eyelids. Red lipstick and gold-flecked eye shadow came off on a handful of tissues which she then flushed down the toilet. There could be no lingering reminders of Amber in this house. This is where Amelia lived.

As she stepped out of her sweatsuit and stuffed it in the back of her closet, an owl hooted softly outside her bedroom window, the only witness to Amelia's deceit. Grabbing a nightgown from a hook on the door, she slipped it on, savoring the familiarity of this fabric as opposed to the shiny red satin that she'd worn on the job.

No sooner had her head touched the pillow than her eyes closed. Aware that she sighed, it was the last thing she heard until morning when Aunt Wilhemina's voice echoed loudly up the staircase.

"Ahmeelya! It's past time to get up. You'll be late for work."

Amelia groaned and rolled out of bed. It was her own fault that she felt like hell, but if her plan worked, it would be worth it.

When she'd first come to live with her great-aunts, Wilhemina and Rosemary Beauchamp, she'd been a skinny, too-tall nine-year-old and they, the only living relatives that could be found after her missionary parents were killed in a Mexican earthquake.

Amelia had been used to living rather freely from country to country—from custom to custom. The culture shock she experienced when she came to live with two old-maid aunts was similar to the shock they received when she arrived. But the Beauchamps were nothing if not proper, and what was right was right. Kin was kin. Here she was. Stay she must. So they began to mold her into a smaller, younger replica of themselves and thus began the starching of Amelia Ann.

Yet in spite of their persistence, she managed to retain most of her own personality during elementary and secondary schools. She even managed to exhibit some independence during her college years in nearby Savannah. She'd kept a fairly normal social life during that time, which had even resulted in one serious suitor who'd lasted clear up to the time she introduced him to the aunts. After that, things were never the same between them.

Amelia supposed that he'd looked into the future, seen the responsibilities of not only a wife but two elderly females to look after, and bolted. She'd been mildly devastated at the time, but it had passed sooner than she would have liked. Her suitor had absconded with love, her trust in men *and* her virginity. It took the heart right out of her independence.

She was unaware that with the passing of time, she'd begun dressing like her aunts, acting like them and even had a future mapped out by them. And time had done her another rare favor. Her broken heart had completely healed and her trust in men in general was normal. The only thing that could never be returned was her virginity. In some small measure, she was glad. She would hate to die an old maid—*and* a virgin.

It was the realization of that same passing time that had prompted her secret rebellion. Amelia could see herself, twenty, thirty, even forty years down the road—in this same house—in the same town—wearing the same style of clothing—and alone. Always alone! She loved her aunts dearly, but she had no intention of ending up like them. She wanted adventure and excitement. She wanted to be able to get out of Tulip should the mood arise.

That's why she needed the new car. On a librarian's salary, such things were impossible. As far as the Beauchamp sisters were concerned, their old, blue Chrysler sufficed. Amelia had other ideas. She could not see the world in a 1970 Chrysler.

Aware that Aunt Witty would be shouting her name a

second time if she did not hurry, she headed for the bathroom. In no time she was dressed, having chosen a sedate shirtwaist dress from her closet and ignoring the fact that beige was not her best color.

Last night's face that she'd worn with secret delight, the one that had laughed and teased and dared to be different, was gone along with the flowing, chestnut mane of hair. In its place was staid propriety.

She brushed her hair a vigorous one hundred strokes then slid her fingers deftly through the nearly unmanageable length and soon had it wound into a thick brown crown. The only thing that adorned her face was a slathering of moisturizer and a hint of the palest, pink lipstick. She slid dark, owl-rimmed glasses over the bridge of her nose and sighed as she headed down the stairs. It was time for Miss Amelia to begin her day as librarian of Tulip, Georgia.

"Sit, girl," Wilhemina ordered, as she laid a warmed plate at Amelia's place and pushed a platter of fluffy biscuits in her direction.

With full intent of only having juice, Amelia pushed her plate aside. "No thanks, Aunt Witty. I'm not really hungry."

Wilhemina Beauchamp raised an eyebrow. It was enough to persuade Amelia to reposition her plate and sit. As she reached for a biscuit, she grinned at Aunt Rosie who was dawdling over her second cup of coffee and staring blankly out of the drawing room window at the butterflies kissing the tops of the blue bachelor buttons in the garden below.

"Morning, Aunt Rosie," she said, as she chewed.

Rosemary blinked at the intrusion into her daydreams and them smiled when she noticed her niece had come to breakfast.

Wilhemina gave Amelia's dress and hair the once-over and then reprimanded her niece for bad manners. "Don't talk with your mouth full," she said.

"Do hush, Willy!" Rosemary muttered, patting her beloved niece on the arm as she pushed the jar of homemade peach conserve toward Amelia. "For once, let the girl eat in peace."

"If I've told you once in the last eighty-odd years, I've told you dozens of time, my name is not Willy."

Rosemary's lower lip jutted. "But Amelia calls you…"

"I know what she calls me," Wilhemina said. "When she was small, my name was such a mouthful that I allowed her to shorten it. And it's your own fault, you know. She always thought you were calling me Witty, not Willy. Now, it's simply too late to change. Habit is a hard thing to break."

Amelia had had enough, both of biscuits and bickering. She pushed back her chair and blew a kiss in their general direction.

"See you all this evening," she called, and then she was gone. Tulip Public Library was waiting.

A tiny spark of excitement kept bubbling through her thoughts as she drove to the library. She was taking the first steps toward changing her future. She didn't look at the fact that going to work as a hostess in a nightclub was not a step, it was a leap. To her, the most difficult thing about the job was putting on that little bit of red nothing three nights a week. It left little to the imagination and too much to the human eye. But the money she was saving was enough incentive to get past the embarrassment.

She hummed to herself as she drove out of the residential area and onto Main Street. A short distance away she turned into the lot and parked beneath twin magnolias marking the spot where Cuspus Albert Marquiside had held off a band of marauding Yankees during *The War*.

Sometime during the 1920s the Marquiside family had insisted on a brass marker to commemorate their illustrious ancestor's bravery. The marker had long since turned a sickly shade of green and the family name had all but died out. Rumor had it that they'd gone north during the Great

Depression of the thirties, but no one in Tulip would believe it. After all, a true southerner would rather starve to death than go live with Yankees.

Amelia grabbed her purse and her lunch and gave Cuspus Albert's marker a friendly pat as she walked by. It was time for the day to begin.

Tyler Savage turned off Main Street and headed down Magnolia Avenue toward the post office. His suntanned hands were strong and sure as he gripped the steering wheel of his pickup truck. Thanks to Raymond Earl's timely assistance, he was now back in business and mentally calculating the amount of fertilizer he needed to pick up when he was forced to brake sharply and then stop.

Ignoring the fact that she'd just jaywalked in the middle of a through street, Effie Dettenberg scurried in front of Tyler's truck, glaring back only after reaching the safety of the curb. Well aware of his "bad boy" reputation and what some of the more staid members of Tulip's society thought of him, he grinned and winked, then waved as he drove away, unaware that someone other than Effie was also watching him.

Amelia stacked the books that she'd just removed from the book drop and tried not to stare at the man behind the wheel. She knew it wasn't proper, but Tyler Dean Savage required more than a casual glance, and she was still thanking her luck that she'd escaped last night undetected.

Still, he *was* six-plus feet of the most desirable hunk of man to ever come out of Tulip, Georgia. Straight black hair that was as unruly as his reputation; blue eyes that were constantly smiling, even when that sexy mouth was not. From the time she'd been old enough to notice, Tyler Savage and his bad-boy image had never been far from her dreams.

She sighed. Why are all the good-looking ones such rakes? But there was no one to answer her question, and it wouldn't have mattered anyway. Men like Tyler Savage didn't notice women like Amelia Beauchamp.

She picked up the books, shifting them to a more comfortable position, and smiled at Effie Dettenberg as she gained safe footing on the sidewalk.

"Morning, Miss Effie, you're out early."

Effie plastered one wrinkled, bony hand across her shapeless breasts in high dismay as if she'd barely escaped the wrath of hell. "Did you see him?"

"See who, Miss Effie?"

"That Savage boy! He nearly ran me down! People like him shouldn't be allowed to roam at will." She cast a watery eye toward the disappearing brake lights of the red-and-white pickup truck and pursed her lips.

Amelia tried not to smile. In her opinion, that *boy,* who was over thirty years old, was well into prime manhood.

"Now, Miss Effie, I saw him slow down, and you know it."

Effie Dettenberg sniffed loudly. "Well! He still shouldn't be allowed out with his reputation and all." She lowered her voice and looked over her shoulder, just to make sure she wasn't being overheard. "You know what they say about those Savages!"

Amelia tried to ignore the lurch her heart took, but it was useless. Whatever *they* had to say about Tyler Savage was always of interest to her. "No ma'am, I can't say as I do."

Effie's voice was just above a whisper. "They say that his people were smugglers. And…" she took a deep breath and readjusted her gold-rimmed eyeglasses on the bridge of her beaky nose "…they also say that those same smugglers cohorted with Indians. That accounts for that devil-black hair and those sharp cheekbones. That's what they say."

Amelia hid a smile behind her armful of books. "But Miss Effie, that was nearly two hundred years ago. He can't be blamed for whatever his ancestors may or may not have done. Surely you have more Christian forgiveness in your soul than to hold that against him?''

Effie fiddled with her handbag and stared back down the street, half expecting that man to come swooping down upon them and carry them away into the swamps. Effie Dettenberg had a vivid imagination.

"Well, maybe not," she muttered. "But there's no denying that he's a rounder. You mark my words, Amelia Beauchamp, stay away from men like him. He's trouble with a capital *T*."

"Yes, ma'am," Amelia said and ignored the sinking feeling in her stomach. Unfortunately for her, he posed no threat. "Come inside the library, Miss Effie. I've just received one of those craft books that you like. It had the most darling crocheted shawl on the cover."

That changed the subject and got Effie off the streets, but it was another thing altogether to get Tyler off Amelia's mind.

The clock chimed six times in succession as Amelia fidgeted with her fork. She had less than three hours to get the aunts into bed and catch her ride to the nightclub with Raelene Stringer. Thoughtlessly scraping at the streak of chocolate left on her dessert plate, she winced as it screeched loudly into the silence of the room. The aunts would have a fit if they knew she was not only working in the same establishment with Tulip's "loose woman," but that she was riding back and forth to work with her, as well.

Wilhemina frowned. "Amelia, don't scrape your plate! Surely I've taught you better manners than that!"

"Yes, ma'am," she muttered, and sighed as her fork clattered against the Spode.

A frown wrinkled the tissue-thin skin on Rosemary's forehead. "Oh pooh, Willy, you fuss too much. It's not good for the digestion. I read where people actually got ulcers from unpleasant meals."

Wilhemina gasped. "My meals are never unpleasant!"

"I didn't say your cooking was...I simply meant that sometimes you can be..."

Amelia interrupted, anxious that a sisterly squabble not break out now and slow down their evening ritual. She was on a tight enough schedule as it was. "Never mind, you two."

The sisters glared at each other as Amelia jumped to her feet and began gathering the dirty china from the table. "I'll do dishes. Why don't you retire to the parlor and turn on the television. It's nearly time for your favorite show."

Rosemary's rosebud mouth puckered with anticipation, wrinkling the faded blush of her complexion. She clapped her hands and patted her Gibson-girl hairdo back into a semblance of order. "Goody! I just love the 'Wheel.' Maybe someday I'll go to California and be on the show. That Pat Sajak has the nicest smile. He reminds me of..."

Wilhemina frowned. "Don't be absurd! That show is next to gambling and we don't gamble. And..." She fixed her younger sister with a pointed stare. "California is a long way off. We'd have to fly...and we don't fly."

"Of course we don't," Rosemary muttered, as she exited the dining room. "Only birds fly. I swear, Willy. I think you're getting senile. I read the other day where..."

Her sister's jaw jutted dangerously. "I'm not senile...and you read too much."

Amelia sighed. Casting another nervous glance at the clock, she began stacking dishes with a vengeance as the sisters disappeared into the living room.

A couple of hours later, she was fidgeting in her chair and trying not to watch the clock, wondering if they were ever going to go into their rooms. To her relief, Aunt Witty appeared at the head of the stairs wearing a bathrobe wrapped around her tall, spare frame like a faded blue pencil with wrinkles. A long gray braid hung over her shoulder and down across her flat chest, nearly lost in the garment's loose folds.

"Amelia, aren't you coming up?" she called down. "It's nearly eight-thirty."

The aunts were firm believers in the early to bed, early to rise philosophy and never veered from their routine. Amelia bit her lower lip. She hated lying, but she hated being afoot worse. She was going to buy that new car or know the reason why.

"No, Aunt Witty, not yet. I want to finish this book first. I'm at a really good part and don't want to stop."

Wilhemina frowned. She didn't have to look to know that Amelia was probably reading another romance. They were her favorites.

"You've got to quit reading that trash. It will only confuse you. I recommend *Little Women*. It was always a favorite of mine and quite wholesome, you know."

Amelia rolled her eyes. "Yes, ma'am. I'll remember that."

Aunt Witty's door went shut just as Amelia looked up at the clock. She had less than thirty minutes to meet Raelene Stringer.

With a sigh, she marked her place and tucked the book down between the cushions, then dashed to the downstairs closet. She pulled out a small overnight bag and a pair of running shoes. Everything she needed for her job was inside. With one last glance up the darkened stairwell, she turned out the lights and quietly locked the front door behind her.

The streets were nearly empty. Amelia breathed a constant prayer that she would not have to explain her strange mode of dress and behavior, and headed for the corner two blocks over.

The dark gray sweatsuit she was wearing blended into the evening shadows as she jogged to her destination. It was Thursday night and nearly time for Amber Champion to clock in at The Old South outside of Savannah. To her everlasting appreciation, Raelene was waiting for her at the corner of Fifth Street and Delaney.

She giggled as Amelia slid into the passenger seat. "Ooowee, honey, I didn't think you were coming," then she turned on the headlights and put the car in gear. The engine rattled and knocked, a sure sign of something in need of repair.

Once Amelia had gotten the job at The Old South, her excitement had fizzled when she'd realized that getting to work was going to be a problem. Bus service between Tulip and Savannah was sporadic.

Raelene had taken one look at the tall, leggy woman coming out of the boss's office and nearly swallowed her gum. The town librarian had been the last person she would have expected to walk into a place like The Old South.

The club was a hopping nightspot. Many of the men had a way of assuming that just because a woman worked at a place like this, that she was available for more than serving drinks. Of course, Raelene never minded their assumptions. She met some of her favorite men this way. But she recognized Amelia. And she'd never let on when Amelia had been introduced to her as Amber Champion. She simply cocked an eyebrow, shifted her chewing gum to the other side of her jaw, and offered *Amber* a ride. That a friendship of sorts had formed still surprised them both.

Amelia winced as the car belched smoke before smoothing out into its regular gait. Just what she needed. If Raelene's car blew up on Tulip's main street, it would be all over. She was supposed to be safely inside the house immersed in a book of romance.

To her relief, the car seemed to settle, and it was time for Amber to make her appearance. She pulled down the sun visor, adjusting the small mirror on the back, and then began sorting through her bag for makeup and trading eyeglasses for contact lenses.

Raelene eyed Amelia's chestnut curls enviously. "Girl, I don't know why you hide your pretty face behind those glasses. I tried to get my hair that color once and it came out as brassy as that bedstead in the display window at Murphy's Furniture. And those eyes of yours! Lord have mercy, you oughta wear contact lenses all the time. Not everyone has eyes like yours. I don't think I ever knew anyone who had blue-green eyes."

"My daddy did," Amelia said, pausing for a moment to let Raelene maneuver across the old bridge outside of town. It was difficult enough to put on makeup between bumps in the road. That planked bridge was impossible. "And I wear glasses because they are easier. Aunt Witty says they make me look professional."

Raelene rolled her eyes. "Shoot, they just hide those pretty eyes and add about ten years to your age is all. If you have to wear them, you oughta get you some real stylish ones. I saw a picture…"

Amelia smiled and let Raelene talk. It didn't matter what she said because Raelene didn't expect an answer. Before she knew it, they had arrived.

Cars were already beginning to fill the parking lot. It would be a busy night. "We're here," Raelene said, as she turned off the highway.

Amelia began stuffing things back into her bag and gave her hair one last fluff. "We'd better hurry. Tony will have a fit if we're late tonight."

They jumped out of the car on the run.

"So, Tyler, what do you think? If you contract next year's peanut crop to me, you're bound to come out ahead. Regardless of how the price fluctuates at harvest, you're guaranteed a substantial profit."

Tyler grinned. Seth Hastings was a whiz at the commodity markets. And the fact that his father owned one of the larger mills in the area didn't hurt his standing, either.

"Yes, Seth, I suppose I might make a real killing, unless my crop fails and I have to go somewhere and buy someone else's whole damned harvest just to fulfill my contract to you."

Seth Hastings looked over his steepled fingertips to the man sitting on the other side of his desk. "Now, Tyler, you know that's not going to happen. You're one of the best farmers in the state. You haven't had a failed crop since you started wearing pants with zippers."

"I've come too damned close too many times to take anything for granted and you know it," Tyler argued. And then he leaned back in his chair and cocked one long leg across his knee. "But, I'm going to take a chance. I've got a hunch about the government pay base this year and it doesn't feel good. If we don't get someone in office up in Washington that understands farmers and makes some changes in the agriculture program, we're all going to be out on our ears and that's a fact."

"All right." Seth grinned and clapped his hands. "This calls for a celebration! And I know just the place. Ever been to The Old South?"

Tyler glanced down at his watch, calculating the time he knew that they'd spend at some club against the time he had to drive home to his farm outside of Tulip, and decided that he deserved a break.

"No, but I have a feeling I'm about to be taken there."

"Like Sherman took Atlanta," Seth said.

Tyler grinned. "You better not say that too loud around here."

Seth laughed. "Come on reb, let's go have us a party."

"Lead on, Yankee," Tyler retorted. "I'm due some R and R."

Amelia glowed beneath the subdued lighting like a fire-cracker on the Fourth of July. Her tall, shapely body was neatly encased in shiny red satin and spandex. Lorna, the lifeguard at Tulip's public swimming pool had a suit just like it, only it didn't sport a black net bustle that bounced back and forth as she walked and her legs weren't nearly as long or encased in black fishnet hose like "Amber's".

Trying to ignore the slick touch of a man's hands on

the back of her thigh as she scooted between the tables of customers, she looked down and glared. "I'll be right with you, sir."

He leered back. "I'll be waiting."

Stifling the urge to dump her tray of drinks in his lap, she continued to the next table.

Seth looked up and then whistled softly as he and Tyler were being seated in a darkened corner of the club. "Ooowee."

Tyler followed his friend's gaze and started to laugh when he saw the woman in red...her long, long legs...and that damned bobbing bustle...and forgot to take his next breath. He watched her neatly take command of an unruly situation, take a patron's order and dodge grasping hands without misplacing that smile on her face.

To his dismay, the room began to sway, and he grabbed hold of the table to settle his world. It would be hell if he fell on his face before he ever learned her name. He went from interest to lust so quickly he caught himself shifting uncomfortably in his seat. He hadn't been *this hard this fast* since his sixteenth birthday when Kissy Beth Syler had skinny-dipped in front of him just for kicks. And then he grinned to himself, remembering that she wasn't the only one who'd gotten her kicks that day. He'd had a soft spot for farm ponds ever since. It was a memorable way to celebrate one's arrival into manhood.

"That's one fine-looking lady," Seth murmured.

Tyler's eyes narrowed. Fine didn't begin to describe his opinion.

And then Seth's grin widened as he nudged Tyler's leg beneath the table with the toe of his shoe. "Hey great, she's coming this way. It looks like we lucked out tonight, my friend. We're sitting at one of her tables."

"What'll you gentlemen have?"

Amelia stood with pen poised above paper, staring at a point just to the left of the men's shoulders. She never actually looked them in the eye. It was her way of retaining what she considered anonymity. But she need not have bothered. She was as far removed from Amelia Beauchamp's persona as diamonds were from coal.

The man with his back to the wall mumbled something totally unintelligible, forcing Amelia to look up. Her heart thumped wildly as sweat broke out on the back of her neck.

Their gazes locked. Tyler looked up into eyes so green they looked wet and then he blinked. No, maybe they were blue. He could swear he saw sky. He watched her turn pale beneath the layer of makeup she was wearing. A glimpse of pearly white teeth slipped down across her lower lip and Tyler frowned as he watched the pressure increasing. If she wanted her lip bit, he'd be glad to oblige.

Amelia groaned. *Oh my God. I knew that this might happen! Now what in the world am I going to do? If he goes back to Tulip and tells, I'm ruined! Why him? And why now?*

Here he was, the man of her dreams sitting less than a foot away, and she had to fight the urge to run. At this point, the band swung into a loud jazzy number that made hearing nearly impossible. She leaned forward.

"Excuse me, sir, but I didn't hear your order. What did you say you wanted?"

As she leaned, both men got a better than average look at a tightly encased bust threatening to spill from strapless red spandex.

The room took another tilt as Tyler realized he had the strangest urge to lay this woman down beneath their table and peel that red stuff off of her a little bit at a... To his dismay, he verbalized his thoughts.

"Want? I want you!" *Oh, good God. What did I say?* "Uh...I mean, I want you to excuse me. Seth, you order. I've got to...I need to...where's the...?"

Amelia breathed a sigh of relief. He didn't recognize

her. "First door on your left down the hall," she said, and then waited to get their order as Tyler strode away from the table.

Tyler leaned over the sink, splashing his face with cool water, although it wasn't the part of his anatomy that needed cooling off. He stared blankly at the water droplets running down his face and absently blotted them with a handful of paper towels.

"What in hell just happened to me?"

But his reflection didn't answer. From the looks of it, his reflection was just as scared as he was. This didn't look good, but that woman surely did. He tossed the towels into the trash and headed out the door.

Seth shoved a tall glass of cola in front of Tyler. "Are you all right? I didn't think you needed anything alcoholic. You looked like you were getting sick."

He shrugged, unwilling to admit how she'd rattled him. "I'm okay. I don't know what…"

Something lacy and black caught the corner of his eye. Perfume wafted across his nostrils. Even in this din, even through the smoke, he smelled her coming.

Amelia walked up behind him and set a small dish of peanuts on the table to go with their drinks.

When her arm came across his line of vision, he jumped as if he'd been shot.

Already nervous at being in such close proximity to a walking disaster, Amelia leaned down once more, shouting to be heard. "I'm sorry. I didn't mean to startle you."

Tyler stared, once again lost in those blue-green eyes and that cloud of chestnut curls drifting around her face. If she bit her lip again he was in serious trouble.

"That's all right, miss…?" Seth Hastings waited with a smile on his face, expecting her to fill in the blanks with her name. She obliged.

"My name is Amber," she answered. "Will there be anything else?"

Her name is Amber! Tyler grabbed her arm. "Yes."

She waited, and then waited some more as his fingers tightened around her wrist. She began to panic again. What if he was beginning to…? And then he shouted in her ear.

"Bring me some nuts."

Seth's grin widened perceptibly, which did not help Tyler's unraveling composure.

Amelia looked at him as if he'd grown horns and carefully pushed the dish toward him that she'd just placed on the table.

He looked down at the salty, brown nuts and reluctantly let go of her wrist.

"Oh…uh, thanks."

Seth rolled his eyes. This was getting better by the minute.

"Will there be anything else?" Amelia asked. She was almost afraid to wait for the answer.

"If there is, we'll yell," Seth said. "And thanks…Amber. You're a doll."

Tyler frowned. He didn't think he liked the fact that Seth just paid the woman a compliment. He grabbed his cola and downed it in one gulp, watching that bobbing bustle over the rim of his glass as Amber walked away.

Seth grinned. "Old girlfriend?"

"I wish," Tyler muttered, and then grinned back at his friend's owlish leer. "Just shut the hell up, Seth. I haven't signed that contract yet. If you keep this up, I still may not."

Seth pursed his lips into a comical expression of propriety and calmly lifted the bowl of nuts from the table.

"Here you go, Tyler, have a peanut."

Two

___

It was almost closing time, and without doubt, the evening had been the longest of Amelia's life. The relief of knowing that Tyler Savage hadn't recognized her had left her weak and shaken. It was her first close call since she'd started living a double life.

She fidgeted with the top of her suit as she gathered up her gear. With one last tug at its too-snug fit, she emptied her tips onto the bar and began to count. At least one good thing was coming out of this deceit. Her car fund was growing. At the other end of the bar, Raelene was performing a similar routine while employees began to clean up.

And then a voice in Amelia's ear made her jump. Her suit slipped a notch as she whirled around. Openmouthed, she clutched her suit with one hand and a wad of bills with the other as Tyler Savage leaned forward and poked a dollar bill lightly into the crevasse between her breasts.

"You dropped this," he explained, with an obliging grin.

Amelia gasped, and yanked it out with a flourish. "Thank you," she muttered, and spun around, anxious that he not see her so closely, face-to-face.

"Amber…?"

Her heart skipped a beat as his deep, sexy drawl lingered in her ears.

"What?" she muttered, and began stuffing money into her bag. She had to get away from him and she had to do it now. This situation was making her nervous.

"Would you go out with me sometime? Maybe to dinner…a movie…or dancing, wherever you wanted. You name it."

He waited anxiously for her answer, remembering the hour he'd spent after Seth had gone home just watching her wait tables. For some strange reason, she didn't seem as if she was a stranger, although he knew for a fact that he'd never seen her before tonight.

While he waited for an answer, Amelia went into a panic.

Oh my Lord! He's just asked me out on a date! What do I do? All these years he's ignored my existence and now he decides to notice me? Now when I can't do a darned thing about it? It's not fair! And then it dawned on her that he hadn't really asked *her* out, he'd asked Amber. It was a frustrating and sobering thought.

Of course, had Amelia been honest with herself, she would have admitted that her own personal appearance had nothing to do with Amber's. As Amelia she'd done nothing to attract his, or any other man's attention. It wasn't entirely Tyler Savage's fault that he didn't know Amelia Beauchamp existed. But as Amber, she didn't have to do anything to attract attention. Her pretty face and that shiny red suit were enough enticement for any man with the inclination.

"We don't know each other," she muttered, as she

stuffed the last of her tips away. "I don't think that a date would be proper."

Tyler couldn't believe what he'd heard. He'd expected any number of answers, but a concern about propriety had not been one of them. In his experience, propriety and barmaids had little in common.

He leaned forward, just shy of touching her again. "We'd get to know each other a whole lot better if you'd agree to go out with me."

Amelia groaned. His voice was as compelling as the man himself. She closed her eyes and then shuddered. There was no way on God's earth that she could go out with him. He might suspect, and if he did, she was ruined. With a dejected sigh, she looked up.

"Thanks all the same," she said softly, "but I don't think it's such a good idea."

Tyler died in her eyes and was resurrected by the smile on her lips. Her mouth was moving. He knew it because he could feel her breath against his face, but focusing on her words was impossible. And then she started to walk away.

"Does this mean no?"

Another soft smile slid into place in spite of her intention to remain aloof. "It means just what I said, mister. It's not a good idea." In fact, you have no idea how dangerous it would be.

"My name is Tyler…Tyler Savage. And I'm real good at changing people's minds."

At that, he reached out and gently tucked a stray curl back in place that had been teasing at the corner of her eye.

Amelia held her breath as his finger stroked against her temple. She was afraid he wouldn't stop with a touch and afraid that she wouldn't have the guts to say no again.

Tyler ached to hold her. The lost, almost vulnerable look that kept appearing and disappearing on her face was nearly his undoing. As aloof as she seemed, he sensed insecurity and fear were the true reasons for her behavior.

"Okay, you win…this time. But I'll be back, and I'll need a better excuse than the one you used tonight. Okay?"

Amelia let out a pent-up sigh as she watched him walk away. "Well, I never," she muttered, and then realized that was just what was wrong with her. Or at least she hadn't for a long time. If she had…at least recently…she wouldn't be so hesitant to take the man up on an offer she'd been praying would come.

"Ooh, honey," Raelene muttered. "Why did you let that one get away? You know what they say about him, don't you?"

"Him, who?" Amelia had to play it safe and pretend that they'd just met. It wouldn't do to admit that she'd spent the better part of the past eight years of her life transposing Tyler's face onto the heroes in her romance books.

Raelene stared. This woman floored her. She'd never understand what was going on inside that head. She knew good and well who Amber really was. She also knew that "Amber" had to know who Tyler Savage was. He'd lived in Tulip his entire life. Nevertheless, this wasn't her game to play. So instead of arguing the issue, she shrugged and pointed.

"Him…Tyler Savage. He's one hunk of man and if the stories about him are true, one hot lover, too."

Amelia groaned and wished she was physically able to kick herself in the rear. It boggled the mind that she'd turned him *and* his reputation down. Her shoulders drooped as she stared at the empty doorway through which he'd disappeared.

"Oh, I've heard all of that, but so what if it's true? He wouldn't be interested in me." For the first time since her and Raelene's relationship had begun, Amelia as good as admitted she was a fraud. She met Raelene's knowing gaze. "Not the *real* me, anyway."

Raelene grinned. "There's more to the real you than I think you're willing to admit." She wiggled her eyebrows, and her hips wiggled in unison as if they were somehow connected.

Amelia laughed at her friend's honesty while being secretly disgusted with herself for not being as sincere. She was desperate to go out with Tyler despite the fact that he might recognize her. She also knew that it wasn't fear of being recognized that kept her from accepting him. It was fear of what *she'd* lose if she did. He was the kind of man who took women's hearts and then kept them.

Raelene patted her on the arm. "Come on, honey. Let's call it a night."

A short while later, a stray dog barked at Raelene's car as it entered Tulip. It belched to a stop two blocks over from the Beauchamp residence.

Amelia winced. "Thanks for the ride, and I guess I'll see you tomorrow."

Raelene yawned and then grinned wearily. "Honey, it's already tomorrow."

"How true," Amelia said, and then bolted from the car, trading the sidewalks for the darker, less obvious alleyways, as she headed for home.

In no time, she'd entered the house, breathing a quiet sigh of relief as she locked the front door behind her. Once again, another night of deception had passed undetected.

Yet her conscience would not let her forget that tonight, for just a moment, she'd thought the charade was over. Because of it, a man whom she'd dreamed of for years had asked her out and she'd had to say no.

But, he didn't ask *me,* Amelia fumed. He asked that damned Amber.

She didn't even wonder about the futility of being envious of her own self. She was too frustrated and weary.

And she thought she might be coming down with something. There was a strange ache hanging around her heart.

Tyler pulled a clump of peanuts from the ground, searching the underside of the leaves for signs of leaf spot. He pinched at the small, immature nuts hanging like little ornaments on the ends of the plant roots, checking constantly for nematodes as well as the size of the kernel inside the soft shell, hoping that he didn't find more pops than nuts.

He'd paid to have the crops sprayed just last week and crop dusters didn't come cheap. He looked up at the clear blue sky and the tufts of gathering cumulus clouds, shading his eyes beneath the brim of his cap and searching the far horizon for the impending signs of rain that the weatherman had promised earlier this morning.

He began to walk the rows, oblivious to the irrigation system in operation. His long legs moved in rhythm to the pulsing jets of water spraying his body and the crops. He was concerned with the tiny, dark green clumps of peanut plants aligning themselves in perfect unending order down the fields.

Beneath the soil, a bountiful harvest was growing, feeding itself from the rich nutrients in the Georgia loam. And yet for the first time in his life, he felt no satisfaction in the knowledge that he was standing on money in the ground. All he could think about was sundown. And a nightclub outside of Savannah called The Old South. And a woman called Amber.

"Hey, boss," a man yelled. "You want us to shut this down?"

Tyler looked up in surprise. For a moment, he'd actually forgotten where he was. He waved to the man in charge of the irrigation crew.

"May as well," he said, looking up at the sky with a practiced eye. The building thunderheads were a promising sign of rain. "Give it a rest. Weatherman said rain tonight and if it comes a good one, maybe we won't have to water the fields for a while.''

"You're the boss," Elmer said. And did as he was told.

"Some boss," Tyler mumbled to himself. "I'm not even in charge of my good sense. Damn stupid that I'm trying to run this farm, too."

"What did you say?" Elmer asked.

"Oh, hell, Elmer," Tyler laughed. "Ignore me. I'm just talking to myself."

Elmer laughed. "Yeah, farming will do that to you. I'll tell you what's wrong with you, though. You need to get you a woman."

When Tyler grinned, Elmer held up his hands in surrender. "Not that kind of woman, Ty. You need one to come home to. You're past thirty years old and still unmarried. Dammit man, we need to get you out of circulation. I got a daughter who giggles every time you drive by. I'd hate like hell to have to whip your ass when she turns twenty-one. You need to get yourself involved."

An image of a tall, voluptuous woman in tight red spandex flashed before his eyes. The last thing he was interested in was one of Elmer Tolliver's moony-eyed daughters. Tyler was already involved. He just had to find a way to convince Amber to participate.

Raelene gasped and then nudged Amelia sharply beneath the ribs. "Ohmigod! Would you look at that? He's back! You're gonna have to break down and put that man out of his misery, girl. What is it now...four...five times he's been back?"

Amelia sighed, trying to ignore the way her heart raced and her stomach tied itself into little knots every time that man entered the room.

"Six," Amelia muttered. "And wouldn't you know it. He's at one of my tables again."

Raelene laughed. "Well hell, honey. Why do you think he comes here? It can't be for the company. He sits at that table by himself all night and watches you walk. That's why he's here." She laughed again at her own wit as she fluffed Amelia's bustle. "So go on out there and give him something to remember."

Amelia glared at her friend and tried not to wiggle as she walked across the floor to take his order. But it was impossible to stop the motion where her body was concerned. What didn't sway, bounced. "What'll it be?" she asked. Pen poised above her order pad.

"You know what I want," he said softly. "But in the meantime, you can bring me a soda."

"You could get a soda at any corner quick stop."

"Yeah, but the service isn't near as pretty. Hank's missing two teeth, and his overalls don't fit nearly as well as your outfit. I'm a bit prejudiced toward short...skintight... black net...shiny red..."

Amelia made a beeline for the bar.

Listening to him flirt was getting to be a bit painful. His voice pulled at secret places inside her belly. His eyes taunted her body to react in the most embarrassing of manners. He was wearing her down and they both knew it.

She slammed her tray onto the bar and almost shouted out her orders. The bartender actually forgot to make a wisecrack as he hurried to complete her requests. Amelia leaned her forehead onto the palm of her hand and closed her eyes with regret.

"Sorry," she said, as he set the drinks onto her tray. "It's been a long week."

He nodded and smiled.

Amelia lifted her tray and then turned, staring through the dimly lit room to the table in the back. "That does it! He's driving me crazy. I can't take it anymore. I'm going to put a stop to this.... Now!"

She sailed across the floor, tray held high, dodging hands and sharp remarks as she quickly served the tables their drinks, saving Tyler's order for last.

"Here's your cola," she said shortly. "And you win!"

He nearly forgot to breathe.

"I win?"

Amelia glared. "You know what I mean! Don't play coy with me at this late date, mister." She leaned forward to make her point.

He shoved his drink aside and stood up. Their faces were mere inches apart, their breaths caressing each other's cheeks.

"When?"

She rolled her eyes and slammed her tray against her breasts, unconsciously using it as a shield between them.

"The sooner the better. Then maybe you'll get this out of your system and I can get back to work." But how I'll get you out of my system later is my problem, she thought.

"How about tomorrow night?"

Amelia thought for a moment and then nodded. She started to walk away when his voice stopped her cold.

"Amber?"

She turned.

"I have a small problem."

She waited for him to continue.

"I don't know your last name…or where you live."

Oh God! "Umm…it's Champion. And don't bother picking me up. Just meet me here around nine."

"So late?" Tyler was hoping for more.

"It's that or nothing. I have two jobs. It's impossible to come earlier."

"I'll take it," he said softly. And I'll take you. Anywhere…on any terms.

"Fine then," Amelia muttered. "I have to get back to work now."

His hands cupped her shoulders, lingering on the bare curves before running lightly down to the bend of her elbows. He grasped her gently and shook her to get her attention.

"You won't be sorry, Amber."

I already am, she thought. And then she smiled. She'd

been sorry half her lifetime. What was the matter with her? She'd wanted a change in her life. Dating Tyler Savage was a fine place to start. She comforted herself by thinking if he hadn't recognized her by now, he wasn't going to.

Tyler wondered about the odd little smile that flitted seductively around her lips before disappearing into those wide blue-green eyes. His pulse accelerated as he watched her walk away, lost in the bustle bouncing in rhythm to her long-legged stride. He had a feeling that tomorrow was going to be the best night of his life. If everything went the way he hoped, it might also be the beginning of the rest of it, too.

"Ahmeelya!"

Amelia flew down the front stairs, gasping as she dashed into the dining room. "Yes, Aunt Witty?"

"Don't run. Don't shout. Breakfast is ready. And you're already late."

Wilhemina shoved a warm plate in front of her niece and frowned, running a practiced eye over Amelia's pale pink shirtwaist, frowning even more as she noticed that it picked up too much color from her cheeks. A woman couldn't be flashy. It wasn't ladylike to call attention to one's self.

Rosemary poured herself another cup of coffee and slipped into the chair beside her niece. "My, but you're looking pretty this morning, dear. You remind me of myself when I was a girl. I had more beaus than you could shake a stick at. Why, I remember the time…"

"Hush, Rosemary," Wilhemina said sharply. "You'll give the girl ideas."

Amelia hid a smile. She was twenty-nine years old, not nine. And as for ideas, Tyler Savage had already put more into her head than she could cope with.

"I'll bet you both had your share," Amelia said diplomatically.

Her Aunt Witty's blush came as a big surprise. Almost as much as the fact that she actually smiled.

Rosemary giggled. "Oh, Willy, do you remember Homer Ledbetter? He had the biggest crush on you when you were…"

The smile on Wilhemina's face suddenly pursed. "Oh yes! I remember Homer well. He took Sissy Manion to the school picnic instead of me. I never did forgive him. After all, he'd promised." Her mouth pursed unforgivingly. "Let that be a lesson to you, Amelia. You can't trust men."

Rosemary wasn't to be deterred. "Pooh! Homer Ledbetter wasn't even close to being a man. If I remember correctly, he hadn't been out of knickers more than three or four years. Besides…everyone knew why he took Sissy. She used to let the boys…"

"Rosemary!"

Amelia grinned as she swallowed her last bite of scrambled egg, washing it down with a gulp of juice.

"I've got to go," she said. "Have a nice day, okay? I'll see you both this evening."

"Anyway," Rosemary continued as if there'd never been a breach in the conversation. "If you hadn't been such a persimmon about things, he'd have asked you out again."

"Well, maybe I didn't want him to," Wilhemina argued.

It was the last thing Amelia heard as she made a dash for the car. The ancient Chrysler coughed twice before the motor turned. With an aging wheeze, it came to life as she put it in reverse and backed from the driveway. She could hardly wait for the day when she climbed into a car that belonged to her. One that started with the turn of a key, not on a hiccup and a prayer. And one that would get her farther than Tulip Public Library.

Tyler shifted gears as he drove into town, slowing down in accordance with the speed zone sign that used to be standing at the city limits. The sign had blown away during the last hurricane more than fifteen years ago, but the signpost was still there. It was just understood that the 35 mph limit was still in ordinance.

The wind blew through the open windows of his truck, cooling his sweat-drenched shirt just enough to give it a sticky, clammy feel against his skin. Last night's rain had been a welcome relief, but the day's heat was making the weather just short of unbearable. He glanced down at his wristwatch and made a quick decision. It was already close to noon and he still hadn't made it to the fields. A flat on one of the duals of his 4850 John Deere had changed his plans. It had taken the better part of an hour to wrestle the huge tractor tire off the axle and another ten minutes just to get it into the back of a flatbed truck.

He turned down main street and headed for the filling station, knowing that it would take some time to get the flat fixed. The least he could get out of this morning was a decent meal at Sherry's Steak and Soup. It wasn't gourmet fare, but it beat his own cooking all to hell.

Amelia shifted the phone to her other ear as she leaned over the library counter and turned the sign on the door to read Closed.

"No, Aunt Witty, it's my fault, not yours. I forgot to pick up my lunch this morning. And I know you two have garden club this afternoon. I've already decided to go over to Sherry's Steak and Soup and have a salad." She rolled her eyes as her aunt began a tirade on the dangers of too much fast food and grease. "I said, I'm having a salad. And yes, I'll watch my waist." Although I don't know who besides you two will care.

She grabbed for her purse as she hung up the phone, unwilling to linger over their conversation and give her aunt time to make further suggestions concerning her food.

* * *

Jenny Michaels tucked a pencil behind her ear and shifted her chewing gum to the other side of her cheek. "Hey, Tyler Dean. I haven't seen you in a month of Sundays. Sit anywhere you like. I'll be right with you."

"Just bring me a chicken fry and the works," he said.

"Hey, Cookie, chicken fry with all the trimmings," she shouted from across the room.

Amelia came in the side door and slid onto a bar stool just as Jenny was about to pick up an order from the kitchen. Jenny paused and whipped her pencil out from behind her ear.

"Hey there, Amelia. I'd better take your order before the cook gets bogged down in burgers and fries. What can I get 'ya?"

"A chef salad," she answered. "Oh! And don't forget I want…"

Jenny grinned. "I know. You want your boiled egg quartered. No ham. Only chicken. And fat-free ranch dressing on the side."

Amelia frowned. "Am I in that much of a rut?"

"I don't know," Jenny said and then winked. "Are you?"

"Just bring me my salad," Amelia said wryly. "Save the psychiatrist's couch attitude for someone who needs it."

Jenny leaned forward. "Speaking of couches…there's someone I'd like to get on one."

Amelia turned, her eyes following the direction of Jenny's pencil and then nearly fell off the bar stool as Tyler Savage stared at them from across the room.

Oh God! He's here! What do I do? What if he…? "Don't get in such a snit," she told herself. "Remember…he doesn't know a thing."

Misunderstanding the pep talk Amelia had given to herself, Jenny raised her eyebrows several inches. "That's not what I hear. I hear he knows plenty. And if I had my way, he'd be teaching some of it to me."

Tyler shifted uncomfortably under the force of their gaze. It was blatantly obvious that he was the focus of their conversation. He knew Jenny well, but he couldn't place the woman at the counter. She looked familiar, but she wasn't exactly his type. Her hair was wound up in a tight little knot on top of her head. Even worse, her glasses had long since gone out of style and her makeup was non-existent. And that dress. Lord! His mother used to wear dresses like that. If that wasn't enough, the way she'd ordered her food all sorted out and separate seemed a little prissy. Seemed a big waste of time considering it was all going to the same place.

Jenny elbowed Amelia who quickly turned her back on Tyler's intent gaze. "I think he noticed we were talking about him."

"He'd have to be blind not to. You were pointing."

Jenny shrugged as she turned in Amelia's order and picked Tyler's up to deliver. "Doesn't pay to be bashful, believe me."

Amelia buried her face in her hands, hoping that this meal would pass with no hitches. There was no way he should be able to recognize her as Amber. After all, librarians didn't vamp, they shelved.

Tyler grinned at the waitress as his food was placed in front of him. The aroma was enticing, and so was the thought of tonight. He could hardly wait to get to Savannah and pick up Amber for their night out.

"Be needing anything else?" Jenny asked with a wink. "Anything at all?"

Tyler grinned even wider. He knew Jenny was flirting, but it was a nonthreatening type of flirt and one with which he was very accomplished. "Now if I do, Jen, you'll be the one I'll call."

Jenny smiled and then hurried away.

He dug into his food with relish. Jenny was nice. But she definitely didn't have what Amber Champion had, including long legs, a tight, skimpy red outfit and a pair of the greenest eyes he'd ever seen. Or were they blue? He tried to remember, but it was no use and it didn't really matter. After tonight he'd know a whole lot more about Amber Champion than the color of her eyes.

Three

———

It hadn't been easy to choose a dress for her date with Tyler because the salesgirl kept staring at the dresses Amelia was trying on. They were nothing like the plain shirtwaists that she usually wore, but Amber didn't wear beige shirtwaists and that's who Tyler had asked out on a date.

Amelia turned first one way and then the other, staring at her transformation in the full-length mirror in her room. The dress looked even better than she remembered in the store. Granted it had elbow-length sleeves, a square neckline that was only modestly revealing and a rather unremarkable length to the skirt. It did fall neatly below her knees some two or three inches.

But it was red. And it was tight. And it was nothing Amelia Beauchamp would have been caught dead wearing. However, that point was moot. She hadn't bought it for Amelia. She'd purchased the drop-dead dress for Amber and her date with Tyler Savage.

Getting out of the house dressed like this would be

tricky. It would be even more difficult catching a ride with
Raelene without being seen in a fire-engine red dress, but
she had a plan. Her hair and makeup could be done in the
car on the way to Savannah, just as she did every night
she worked. And she'd wear her all-weather coat over the
dress. It wasn't a good plan. But it was the only one she
had.

The bed frame creaked in the room down the hall while
a floorboard creaked in the one opposite. Amelia sighed
with relief. The aunts were in their rooms and would be
out for the night. There was something to be said for rit-
ualistic routines after all.

Giving herself one last glance in the mirror, she all but
wiggled with anticipation. Now all she needed was a whiff
of perfume, red to match her dress, and the hope that tonight would be all that she'd dreamed.

But when Amelia slipped on her raincoat, she frowned.
It didn't conceal as much of her appearance as she'd
hoped. A good three inches of tight red skirt showed beneath its hem.

Oh well, she reminded herself, if she was lucky, and she
had been so far, no one would even see her. She grabbed
her shoes and made for the stairs, taking them two at a
time in her stocking feet. It was only after she was outside
and on the porch with the front door safely locked behind
her, that she slipped on the slender black sling-back heels
that were a remnant from her college days.

The first star of evening was already out although it
wasn't truly dark. Night air lifted the hem of her coat,
reminding her that haste would be wise. The less seen of
this red dress, the better.

Effie Dettenberg stood on the back stoop of her house,
peering nervously into the evening shadows. Maurice
wasn't home. It wasn't like him to be out so late and she
didn't know what to do. If she called the police, they'd be
angry, just like they were the last time she'd called. But a

woman had rights. She paid her taxes. If she needed assistance, the police were the ones who should come to her rescue.

However, Tulip's finest didn't think much of hunting Miss Effie's black tomcat. Especially during the spring and summer months. They'd tried the best way they knew how to delicately explain to Miss Effie that during this time of year it was a tomcat's nature to do what he did best, and that was to tomcat. It was a known fact that every year several litters of baby kittens in Tulip persistently bore marked resemblances to the wily old tom.

Effie wandered off the porch and into her yard, her gaze fixed on the low hanging bushes surrounding her property. "Here, kitty, kitty, kitty."

And then her voice quavered, ending on a high-pitched squeak as she looked around the corner of her house to the one across the street. Amelia Beauchamp had just slipped out of the house and was standing barefoot in plain sight of God and everybody while she slipped on her shoes. Effie's heartbeat accelerated as Amelia's strange behavior increased. She watched as the young woman looked nervously up one side of the street and down another before darting through the alley opposite the Beauchamp house.

Effie gasped and headed inside, her mind spinning as she ran. If she hurried, she'd just about have time to…

Unaware that she'd been discovered, Amelia hurried through the alley, anxious to get to Raelene. She didn't know what this evening would bring, but it would beat what was between the covers of her favorite romances. This time, she was living one of her own.

And while Amelia was lost in dreams, Effie was adjusting her binoculars to her myopic vision. As she peered down the alley through the magnifying lenses, the world suddenly came into focus. She gasped, bumping her head on the window of her second story bedroom.

Amelia Beauchamp was wearing a red dress, and it was

so tight the girl could hardly walk a decent stride! Effie chewed on her lower lip in frustration as the magnolia trees in the Williams backyard got in her view.

"Fudge," she muttered, while screwing wildly on the binoculars' adjustment, desperately trying to bring Amelia back into sight. "Oh my Lord!" Effie shrieked, and leaned so far out the window, she dropped the binoculars into the birdbath below. "Double fudge," she said, looking down in regret as she rubbed at the sore spot on her head. "I can't believe what I just saw. If I hadn't seen it with my own eyes, I wouldn't have believed it anyway."

Maurice was forgotten as she flopped down on the side of the bed and contemplated the fact that she'd just seen Amelia Beauchamp in a tight red dress and covered suspiciously with a coat when anyone but a fool would know it wasn't even cold. And what was worse, she'd gotten into a car with that trollop, Raelene Stringer.

The implications were many, but facts were few, and Effie Dettenberg prided herself on dealing in facts. For now, she'd remain silent about what she'd seen. After all, she'd known Amelia ever since she'd come to live with her aunts. She was a good girl and had never caused her aunts a day of worry. And, she was a wonderful librarian, always saving the best craft books for her.

Effie fluffed her hair back into place and made her way downstairs to rescue the binoculars, although she knew in her heart that they were ruined.

"But," she reminded herself as she fished the remnants out of the concrete birdbath, "I don't really know what that girl's life was like before she came to live with Wilhemina and Rosemary. I heard…" she told herself, as she started back inside with the pieces tucked safely into her apron that she'd used as a basket "…she was raised all wildlike. In foreign countries, living foreign lifestyles like the heathens who resided there. Who knows what awful things were branded into her soul? Who knows?" she repeated, and slammed and locked the door—for once leaving Maurice to do his catly duty in peace and quiet.

Tyler looked in the rearview mirror again, repeatedly checking his appearance. He'd never been this nervous about a date in his life. Here he was a grown man, well into his thirties, and he was almost sick to his stomach. He grimaced and then smoothed down his hair with his hands as Raelene Stringer's car belched to a stop behind him.

She was here! The door opened, and she emerged from the old gray Chevy like a butterfly from a cocoon. And God have mercy on his soul, but she was wearing the most form-fitting dress he'd ever seen a woman wear and not get arrested. He didn't know whether to lock her up so that no other man would see her, or put her on the hood of his car as an ornament. Pride alternated with jealousy at an alarming rate. He redeemed his sanity in time to crawl from the driver's seat and go to meet her.

Raelene smiled at the look on their faces. This was better than a soap opera any day. ''Hey, Amber, you know what time I leave. If you want a ride home, don't be late,'' and then she disappeared into the club.

Tyler couldn't quit staring. ''You're so beautiful.''

So are you, Amelia thought, but ''thank you,'' was all that she said.

He was a far cry from the work-weary, sweat-stained man she'd seen earlier in the day eating at Sherry's Steak and Soup. His gray slacks looked soft and moved against the force of his legs as he walked toward her. His muscles bunched then released in fluid motion beneath a shirt so white it almost glowed. The strong angles of his face were framed by hair as dark as the night and as thick as the sultry air around them. Amelia had never wanted anything so badly in her life as to reach out and touch the dark tan on his forearms...to see if he was as warm and sun-browned as he looked.

Night moths fluttered madly against the pole lights scattered around the parking lot of The Old South. A soft breeze came up and pulled at the rich abundance of Amelia's hair, lifting it back and then dropping it down onto her shoulders like a teasing lover. Crickets tuned up from the shadows, reminding all who cared to listen that their symphony was about to begin.

Tyler's hands were shaking as he reached out and brushed a wisp of hair from the corner of her lips, jealous of its right to be where he wanted.

"Where are you taking me?" Amelia asked.

To bed! came the thought. "It's a surprise."

Amelia grinned. "I love surprises."

"Then come with me, pretty lady. Your chariot awaits."

Amelia smiled. "It looks like a pickup truck to me."

"Looks can be deceiving," he said, and then winked.

Her smile slipped as she quietly took her seat inside the vehicle.

Oh Tyler, you have no idea how deceiving.

Meanwhile, a voice inside Tyler's head was asking: Now what did I say to wipe that smile off her pretty face?

But when he sat down beside her, the smile had reappeared and he shrugged off the worry. Tonight was bound to be awkward for them both. He didn't know a thing about her except her name and where she worked. All in good time, he told himself as they pulled out of The Old South and headed into Savannah.

In a short span of time, he'd parked. When he took her by the hand and led her toward the Savannah River and the night lights of the busy clubs on the boundary of the riverwalk, she started to smile.

Threading his fingers through hers, he pointed down at the streets paved with ballast stone from old sailing ships. "Careful, it's a rough walk."

As long as he was holding her hand she wouldn't have cared if the surface had been covered with burning coals. And then she happened to look up.

"Oh Tyler!"

The paddle wheeler, *The Savannah River Queen,* was decked out in full regalia. Lights were strung from prow to stern, beckoning the daring to come take a chance in the dark—on the river—at night.

"If you'd rather do something else…" he began, but her clutch on his arm told him no.

"I've never been on a riverboat!" The wonder in her voice made him smile.

The riverboat's whistle was a reminder that haste would be wise. They quickly made their way into the crowd crossing the gangplank and were soon on board, lining the rail along with the other passengers as the boat began to pull slowly away from the shore.

His long arms came around her from behind as he braced them both from the bumping crowds ogling for pictures. She shivered with anticipation as his body cupped protectively against her back.

"Cold?"

The whisper in her ear was soft. But it wasn't a chill that sent shivers flying up her spine, it was an instant flash fire of heat from the impression of his body against hers.

She shook her head. At this moment, speech was impossible.

The crowd soon dispersed from the rail, leaving them alone outside in the dark.

Tyler didn't want to move. As far as he was concerned, the shadows they were in and their near isolation at the stern of the ship were perfect.

Lights from the ship shone down on the massive paddle wheel beside them, illuminating the churning wake it left behind as they moved through the Savannah's murky depths. City noises were muted by the low rumble of the engine and the water spilling down the wheel. Sounds came out of the darkness, only to be lost as they bounced across the river from one shore to the other.

Amelia was transfixed by the magic. Impulsively she

turned in his arms to point out a passing dolphin high-lighted by the ship's lights when the expression on his face blanked the thought from her mind.

Liquid blue and intense with emotion, his eyes glittered darkly as he looked down upon her. With a sigh, he lifted his hands, feathering them up her arms and circling the elegant length of her neck, then combing them through her hair. The ship rocked slightly as they crossed the wake of a passing ship. Amelia staggered and then she was in his arms.

She heard a groan. Unaware of whether it came from him or her, she leaned forward. And then it was too late for second thoughts as his mouth covered her lips and he took what he needed to survive.

Molding herself to his demands, she was still the first to break their kiss and the embrace. Chin resting on his shirtfront, inhaling the rich, musky cologne of the man himself, Amelia felt the contours of his body as it began to change. A little excited, and a little embarrassed, she froze in place.

Tyler was hard as hell and could tell by the way she was standing that she knew it.

"I'm not going to apologize for that," he warned, and took a reluctant step back.

Amelia looked up. The blue-green in her eyes had dark-ened to a deeper shade of jade. Breath came in short, quick gasps as she desperately tried to regain her sense of self, and then she managed a smile.

"You'd better not," she said, trying to mask the hitch in her voice by a nervous laugh. "So, what's next? Is this where I throw myself into the deep dark water, or did you have something a little dryer in mind?"

Tyler laughed. The sound boomed out across the water, deep and unexpected. Amelia hugged herself with delight at the pure joy of the moment.

"Ah, God, she's not only pretty, she's witty, too. How

in hell am I supposed to fight this feeling I have for you, Amber, love?''

Love! Amelia's smile was lost in the shadows. ''Why Mr. Savage, you're not to supposed to fight it, you're supposed to enjoy it.''

With a grin, he hustled her inside to the lounge where there were lights and people and something to drink that would hopefully put out the fire she'd started in his belly.

Reluctant to give up his tenuous hold on her presence, Tyler stared blindly at the blinking sign proclaiming the whereabouts of The Old South. He didn't want to let her go. Not like this. ''Let me take you home,'' he pleaded.

The expression in her eyes was close to panic. ''No! I already told you, it's impossible. Besides, I promised Raelene I'd ride home with her.''

He gripped the steering wheel with fierce determination as he struggled with a new set of worries. She was too adamant for his peace of mind. A thought that had surfaced more than once tonight began to reoccur.

''If you told me the truth about being single, then why are you so damn afraid for me to see where you live?''

She gasped. ''What kind of a person do you think I am? I would never cheat on the man I loved,'' she muttered angrily, all the while acknowledging his right to be wary. ''I'll say this once, and then I'll never say it again. I'm not, nor have I ever been, married.''

He sagged with relief, his voice filled with regret. ''Damn it, Amber, it's just that I don't want this night to end, and if I took you home, it would be an excuse to spend a little extra time with you, that's all.''

''I'll be here tomorrow,'' she reminded him. And then she sighed as she glanced at her watch. ''Or I should say, later today.''

Tyler saw the weary droop to her lips. Only moments ago they'd been smiling. It was his fault that he'd wiped out the night's joy with his jealousy and his distrust, yet it was obvious that Amber had secrets. Maybe when she was ready she'd share them with him, he thought, as he reminded himself that tonight was only their first date. The first, he hoped, of many. With a sigh of regret, he looked up.

"Here comes your ride."

Raelene came bursting out the back door of the club, waving and smiling as she made her way toward them.

Amelia shivered as she slipped her hand across his knee, longing for one last touch. "I guess I'd better go."

He caught her hand and gave it one last squeeze. "I'm sorry."

"You don't need to apologize for anything. I'm the one who's at fault." More than you can ever know.

"Tonight was wonderful," Tyler said. "Thank you, lady, for finally giving in."

Her heart skipped a beat. "I couldn't help it. You're persistent. You're hardheaded. And," her eyes twinkled as she bounded out of the truck before he had time to object. "You're sexy as all get out, Tyler Savage. What's a woman to do?"

Stunned by her words, he watched until she and her laughter disappeared into the night.

Reliving the night's events, it took him twice as long as usual to get home. He missed the turnoff to Tulip once, and the road leading to his farm twice, but finally made it in one weary piece.

Cursing softly beneath his breath, he pulled up in front of his house and turned off the headlights. Even in the dark, miles away from her presence, he could still smell her perfume—hear her laughter—and feel that silky red dress beneath his hands.

He was one giant ache as he got out of his truck and walked slowly up the steps. The front door opened at the twist of a key. The house was dark and quiet, empty and lonesome. For the first time since his folks had retired and moved to Florida, he wished for the sound of their voices.

As he locked the door behind him, his dog bayed once from behind the house. He smiled at the long, lonesome sound.

"Hell of a time to decide to be a watchdog, boy," he muttered, as he took the solitary trek to his bed. "The thief has already come and gone. And she took my heart with her when she left."

Maurice the tomcat came home just as Raelene let Amelia out at the stop sign on the corner. Effie heard the familiar belch of that trollop's car and frowned, fluffing her pillow as she tried to get comfortable again. At her age, it was becoming more difficult.

A mournful, yowling cry echoed through the second-story window and sent her bounding down the stairs as quickly as her old bones would take her. A dog began to bark in a yard two houses over, an echo of her precious Maurice's announcement of arrival.

She opened the door and scooped the wily old cat into her arms. A deep, throaty purr tickled her nose as she buried her face into the sleek, familiar coat. "Maurice, you bad, bad boy, where have you been?"

And then the sight of Amelia's slim figure hurrying barefoot through the alley saved Maurice from further tongue-lashing. Effie clutched the cat against her flat, droopy breasts as she hissed accusingly to no one but herself.

She missed nothing of the form-fitting red dress, the shoes Amelia was clutching in her hands or the coat draped across her arm. "And where have you been, missy, as if I didn't know! You should be ashamed!"

Maurice purred and dug his claws lightly into the front of her nightgown as she held him to her shoulder. With a twist of her wrist, she turned the lock on her door and started back up the stairs. "Yes indeedy...you should both be ashamed."

Across the way, Amelia slid into bed with a sigh of

relief. Tonight had been hectic…traumatic…frightening…
and worth every minute of sheer terror she'd had to endure.
What had happened afterward had been the stuff of which
dreams are made.

She rolled the pillow into a soft little lump beneath her
chin and closed her eyes. Somewhere in her heart, an old
wound from the young man who'd cared too little about
her finally had been closed, sealed and healed by a big
man's laugh and the touch of his hands as well as the
satisfaction of knowing that if she'd only let it happen, she
would be loved.

But the difficulties of that fantasy coming true were
nearly insurmountable, and she knew it. Tonight, for a
short period of time, Amelia had seen heaven through Amber's eyes. She didn't know what it was going to take to
let it happen again, but she'd be damned in hell if she
didn't give it another try.

A soft, gentle snort drifted beneath the crack in Amelia's
bedroom door. She smiled to herself as the moon began
its wayward journey toward the horizon. Aunt Witty would
die if she knew she snored.

"Why, Amelia!" Wilhemina's exclamation of shock
startled Rosemary into slopping her coffee onto the dam-
ask tablecloth.

Rosemary frowned. "Willy, I do declare! You startled
me half out of my wits and made me spill my coffee!"

"That's frightening, Sister. You only had half your wits
to begin with."

Amelia made a fist of her hands beneath the table and
gave what she hoped was an innocent smile as Rosemary
took offense at the slight to her mental acuity.

"I don't think an insult at this hour of the day is in
order," she muttered, picking at a straggling lock that had
escaped the shaky knot she'd made of her hair.

"Here, Aunt Rosie," Amelia said gently. "Let me do
that."

Rosemary smiled as her niece deftly rewound her long gray hair back into the Gibson Girl hairdo she'd worn for most of her life, sliding the pins in place with practiced hands.

"My word!" Rosemary exclaimed as Amelia reseated herself at the table. "I don't think I've ever seen you looking so...why you positively..." She sighed, patted her throat, and shoved the butter toward Amelia. "I'm at a loss for words."

"That's a first," Wilhemina muttered harshly, ignoring her sister's frown of annoyance.

Wilhemina was in shock. She knew what Rosemary had been trying to say. Amelia positively glowed. That's what. And in her estimation, glowing was not ladylike.

"Amelia Ann, what have you done with yourself?"

Amelia ducked her head, relishing the weight of her hair brushing against her neck, instead of being wound tightly onto the top of her head like a little brown crown.

She scooped a pat of butter for her biscuit and pretended disinterest. "Oh, I read in a periodical the other day where people who have extremely long hair sometimes suffer head and neck pains due to the weight of the hair so I thought I'd try wearing mine down for a day or two and see what happens."

Wilhemina frowned. Rosemary's watery blue eyes opened wide, waiting for the other shoe to fall. She was also surprised about the change in her niece's appearance, but she loved every minute of her sister Willy's disapproval. As far as Rosemary was concerned, Willy disapproved of entirely too much.

"Do go on, my dear," Rosemary urged.

Amelia nodded, pretending ignorance of the upheaval her appearance had caused, when in actuality it had taken her the better part of fifteen minutes just to get up the nerve to come downstairs.

"As I was saying, you know how often I have headaches, and you don't want me to cut my hair, so..."

"You read too many trashy novels, that's what does it," Wilhemina accused.

Amelia ignored the accusation. "I have it secured very firmly away from my face. I don't think it will get in the way at all, do you, Aunt Witty? Besides, this way I get to use that pretty tortoise shell clasp you gave me on my twenty-first birthday, remember? I think you said it belonged to your mother."

Wilhemina sniffed. Amelia had her there. She opted for new grounds for complaint. "What I want to know is where did you get that dress?"

Amelia looked down in planned surprise. She knew that the color would throw a monkey wrench into Aunt Witty's idea of sedate, but she'd been ready for this question, too.

"Oh this! You remember how you told me the other day that I needed to get some new shirtwaists? This was on sale. I saved twenty dollars."

Wilhemina frowned. She hated to argue with being thrifty.

"I love the color," Rosemary gushed. "Do you think they have one in my size?"

"You don't wear prints," Wilhemina accused. "You always wear pastels."

"Only because you pick out my clothes," Rosemary accused as her voice rose an octave. She pointed at Amelia. "I like hers. I always liked paisley prints. Momma had a scarf once in blue paisley. Remember? I like Amelia's dress better that this old pale pink one." Her lower lip puffed out in rebellious silence.

Amelia sighed. She'd known that coming home with a paisley print, rich in the colors of fall, might cause problems. The deep earth tones in browns, and the deepest of amber and green had immediately caught her eye. But she hadn't expected it to cause a fight between the sisters. She'd expected to be the one who caught heck.

"I'll check on my lunch hour, Aunt Rosie," she offered. "But I think this one would be too dark for your delicate coloring. Maybe if they have one in your size in lighter colors it would be better. What do you think?''

Rosemary positively preened and then agreed. ''Momma always said I was delicate.''

''Pooh!'' Wilhemina muttered, out of sorts at being left out of the conversation. ''You were never delicate...lazy maybe, but never delicate.''

Before the biscuits and butter began to fly, Amelia intervened. ''I'll check on the dress, Aunt Rosie. And I love being able to wear your mother's clasp, Aunt Witty. It will make my day!''

She leaned over, giving each of the aunts a quick kiss on the cheek as she made a dash for the door. Moments later she was in the old blue Chrysler and backing out of the drive. Tulip's Public Library awaited.

Four

——————

"**H**urry," Amelia called. "We'll be late for services."

Her aunts came down the stairs in a wave of old lavender, rose water and liniment; corset-bound and ruffled, each clutched Bibles against their bosoms, their hair curled and sprayed to perfection.

Wilhemina gave Amelia's choice of clothing the once-over and sniffed approvingly as Amelia retucked her butter-yellow blouse back into a white pleated skirt. "Do you have your Bible?"

"Yes, ma'am." She pointed to the hall table where it and her purse were waiting for an exit. "Come on, Aunt Rosie. I don't want to walk in late again like we did last Sunday. Everyone was already singing when we got to our pew."

The Beauchamp pew was second from the front on the lefthand side, just as it had been since 1899 when Tulip's Southern Baptist Church had been dedicated. At that time, Wilbur Beauchamp had been a young boy of sixteen, and would never have dreamed that he'd one day father the two elderly females now dawdling in the drawing room of the old family home.

"I can't find my hat," Rosemary mumbled. "I had it just the other day. I wonder if I left…"

"It's in the dining room on the sideboard," Wilhemina said with a long-suffering sigh. "I found it outside on the porch swing yesterday afternoon. I swear, Sister, if you had a brain, you'd be dangerous."

Amelia rescued the wide-brimmed, flower bedecked hat and deftly pinned it in place over her aunt Rosie's bountiful hairdo, then rebuttoned the top three buttons on her aunt's dress to take out the kink. She winked at the little woman's complacent smile as she slipped her handbag over her arm.

During the past three years, Rosemary Beauchamp had become increasingly forgetful. Amelia didn't want to think of the implications of such behavior. Right now, she simply wanted to be seated before the pastor began preaching the sermon.

"I'll be waiting in the car," Wilhemina announced, and walked briskly through the open doorway as if going to war.

"I think I'll drive," Rosemary muttered, as she tucked a curl beneath her hat.

Amelia tried not to gape as she grabbed for her own purse and Bible and hustled her little aunt from the porch. "Why don't you let me drive, dear? We're in kind of a hurry this morning, don't you think?"

Completely ignoring the fact that she hadn't driven in over fifteen years, Rosemary considered the suggestion and finally agreed. "I suppose that you're right, dear."

To Amelia's relief, she slipped into the back seat and began fussing with her clothing as if they were going for a long drive instead of three blocks down and one block over.

As they wheeled into the parking lot, the organ music

swelled magnificently, spilling through the open doorway and out into the street. Effie Dettenberg was in fine form.

Effie might be the unofficial town gossip, but she was the official church organist, and she especially loved to play the old hymns like the one she was playing today. "Lily Of The Valley" was a foot-stomping, soul-rousing song from the days when church was held beneath a brush arbor and the preacher nothing more than a self-ordained, reformed rake just passing through.

Amelia struggled to help both aunts up the church steps. With a firm hand beneath each bony elbow, she guided them toward the door. Their goal was just in sight when Rosemary turned on a dime as if she were eight instead of eighty and started back down the steps.

"I forgot my Bible," she said. "I won't be a minute."

"Oh Lord," Amelia gasped, as she caught her by the arm in time to prevent a tumble. "Wait, Aunt Rosie. Let me get it."

Wilhemina gasped and cast a wary eye around, certain that they'd been overheard and their reputation would be in shreds. "Amelia! It's Sunday. Do not take the Lord's name in vain."

Amelia smiled an apology, halted her other aunt's precarious flight, and ran face-first into an all-too-familiar wall of muscle and musk cologne. Strong hands caught her and kept her from falling as she mumbled an unintelligible thank-you while trying not to panic.

Oh no! It's Tyler. He's come to church!

Tyler smiled to himself as he watched matching flags of red sweep across the woman's cheeks. The Beauchamp niece was a strange lady and that was a fact.

"Well good morning, Tyler Dean!" Rosemary cried, and slipped her hand beneath his arm. "I can't remember when I've seen you to speak. How are your momma and daddy doing down in Florida? I've half a mind to go down there myself. Can't stand these winters like I used to."

Tyler's answer was lost to her as Amelia ducked her

head and flew down the steps. Heart thumping in panicked rhythm, she blindly made her way to the Chrysler to retrieve Aunt Rosie's Bible.

Grabbing the woman who barreled into his chest had been reflex, but it was curiosity that made him turn to watch her hasty flight down the steep church steps.

Crisp, white pleats nearly hid the fact that she had exceedingly long legs. And the loose blouse absently tucked into the tiny waistband almost disguised a very voluptuous figure. He wondered why he'd never noticed that about the Beauchamp niece before.

Her ascent back up the stairs was not nearly as swift as the one going down. And it had nothing to do with the fact that she was winded. It had to do with the fact that Tyler Dean Savage stood at the top of the stairs between her aunts, watching her with those clear blue eyes, missing nothing of what she was doing.

"Ms. Beauchamp," he said cordially, smiling to himself at the way Amelia ducked her head when she passed. He wondered why she rolled her hair into that tight wad on top of her head and then wondered why he cared.

"Mr. Savage," Amelia answered. Luckily for her, Aunt Witty was even more anxious to get inside than she.

Wilhemina didn't want to be seen conversing with the town rake. After all, they had their reputation to consider. She led the way into the sanctuary with the others following along behind like a flock of nervous, long-necked goslings.

Amelia slipped into the pew and breathed a quiet sigh of relief, thankful that she'd escaped detection.

But it didn't take long to discover that Tyler Savage was taking more time than he needed to look her way. Several times during the service she caught him watching her with those sharp blue eyes. Once, she even saw his eyes widen and his nostrils flare as if something shocking just occurred to him. She held her breath, closed her eyes and prayed as she'd never prayed in her life. When she looked back up, he'd turned away, seemingly unaware of her existence.

"Thank you, Lord," she whispered, and sank back down onto the pew when the congregation had finished the song.

"That's nice," Rosemary whispered, patting Amelia's knee.

"What's nice, Aunt Rosie?" she asked.

"You thanking the Lord and all." The smile on Rosemary's face disappeared as Wilhemina gave her a sharp jab in the ribs.

"Ouch," she muttered, and glared indignantly at her sister.

"Sssh!" Wilhemina hissed.

They quickly obeyed, forgetting for the moment about savages of any nature.

But from where Tyler was sitting, he had a better than average view of the Beauchamp niece and he was puzzled about the compulsion he felt to keep looking her way. There was something familiar about…!

Sweet Lord! She reminds me of Amber!

Sweat broke out on the back of his neck as he closed his eyes and took slow calming breaths. Church was no place to think about that woman. Now he was going crazy for sure. How he could think that old-maid niece looked like his Amber was beyond him. They couldn't be more diametrically opposed than the South had been to the North during The War.

Only once more did he glance back at the Beauchamp pew, and as he did, again had the strangest sensation of déjà vu. He shook it off, picked up the songbook, and sang along with Miss Effie's rendition of "Near The Cross," unaware that he was nearer to his heaven than he could have imagined.

On the other side of the church, Amelia had come face-to-face with the fact that keeping Tyler Savage in her life might be impossible.

* * *

Ever since the near disaster at church, Amelia had been in a horrible mood. The aunts were well aware of it but had no idea what had spawned her dissatisfaction. Aunt Rosie had plied her with all sorts of favorite treats and Aunt Witty had worried enough to even venture an occasional extra smile. Try as she might, it hadn't been enough to help. Amelia had cried for two nights running. She had a headache that wouldn't quit and knew if she didn't get herself together and make a decision concerning her second life, she knew for a fact that she was going to lose her mind…just like she was losing Tyler.

"Are you through with the grocery list?" Amelia asked.

Wilhemina nodded as she handed her niece the list and a handful of coupons, then patted her awkwardly on the arm.

"It's all we need, but if you see something special that you want, you may get it. Maybe some chocolate fudge ripple ice cream or some marshmallow puff cookies. You know how you used to like those cookies."

Conscience pricked. Amelia knew the aunts sensed her distress. As the days passed, they'd become increasingly upset along with her and because of that, she felt guilty for causing them pain. With a sigh, she wrapped her aunt into a warm, enveloping hug and kissed her weathered cheek.

"Oh, Aunt Witty, I *do* love you," she said. "And I'm fine. I don't need any fudge ripple…*or* those marshmallow cookies. I just need a hug."

Wilhemina returned the hug, along with a guilty look. "I know we're not always as demonstrative you might like, but…"

"Hush, now," Amelia argued. "You're just right. I don't want you or Aunt Rosie to change a hair on your heads. You hear?"

Embarrassed at the unusual show of affection, Wilhemina mumbled. "Well then, you don't need to rush. I won't need the groceries before tonight's meal."

"Yes, ma'am," Amelia said. "See you later."

She left the house with a lighter heart and a determination not to brood any longer. It was obvious that her bad mood had caused her aunts undue worry. Whatever was wrong in her life was no one's fault but her own. There was no need making everyone miserable for what she'd done.

Tyler slammed the door to his pickup truck and then sat with his hands on the steering wheel, staring blindly out across his fields. He hated to even think it, because it might jinx the luck, but it looked as if he was going to have a bumper crop this year. Everything was going smoothly. Even the predicted price per ton for the peanuts beneath those acres and acres of leafy green plants seemed fair.

But it was too much to hope for that his life would be running as smoothly as his farm operation. Amber filled his every waking moment, and too much of his sleeping ones. Yet try as he might, he could come to no solution that would ease his mind and her workload. And the fact that she kept her home life such a secret also weighed heavily. He trusted her. At least he sure as hell *wanted* to trust her. She'd sworn that she had no other man in her life. He had to believe it, and her.

"Get a grip," he reminded himself. Checking his pocket for the list of groceries he needed to purchase, he headed for town.

Effie Dettenberg was studying the labels on similar packages of cookies. One claimed to be *low-fat,* the other, *light.* In her opinion, neither company was telling the whole truth.

"In my day, we didn't need to worry about fat and cholesterol," she told no one in particular as she shoved both packages back on the shelf. "I'll just go home and make a batch of homemade cookies. No need messing with all this. At least if I make them myself, I'll know what's in them."

Effie was so used to telling Maurice her troubles, that she thought nothing of talking to shelves of cookies. It didn't bother her that the cookies didn't answer back. Maurice didn't, either.

And then her eyes narrowed as she spied a familiar figure at the end of her aisle. If she wasn't mistaken, she'd just seen that Amelia Beauchamp. Only this time, she wasn't barefoot or wearing a tight red dress with her hair hanging wantonly around her face.

With a determined smirk, she skewed her shopping cart across the aisle at an angle to mark her spot. She wasn't through shopping down this aisle, and didn't want anyone else getting her place until she was finished with Amelia.

Amelia was studying her list, trying to decide if the cryptic message at the bottom was something Aunt Rosie had wanted her to buy, or if she was simply jotting down the note as a reminder. Aunt Rosie was big on leaving herself notes she never read.

It read, prune, not orange.

To be on the safe side, Amelia decided she'd buy some prune juice, *and* some orange juice.

Effie bustled down the aisle and put herself between Amelia and the jugs of juice.

"Hello, Amelia."

Amelia muffled a sigh. "Miss Effie."

Effie was never one to waste time on small talk. If one had believed in reincarnation, it could have been said that Effie Dettenberg had been an assassin in another life because she went straight for the jugular every time.

"Amelia, I know this is none of my business…"

Amelia rolled her eyes. What ever was?

"But I would have sworn I saw you going up the alley

the other night. I feel obligated to tell you that it's not safe for young women to be…''

All the blood in her body felt as if it had dropped to her feet. Every fear she'd been living with since she'd embarked on this deception just came to life. And of all people to have seen her.

Her voice was calm, but her heart was crashing against her chest like a wild bird trapped in a cage. ''Ummm, are you sure it was me?''

Effie frowned. The twit was going to deny it. ''Well, as sure as I can be, although the Williams' magnolia trees got in the way before I could see exactly whose car you got into. I would have sworn it belonged to that Stringer woman. You know the one….''

Oh Lord, I'm dead! The Williams' magnolia trees? If she saw me get into Raelene's car then that means she must have been watching me with binoculars from her upstairs window!

''I can't imagine what made you think it was me,'' Amelia said shortly.

Possibly because I saw you come right out of your house, Effie thought, but didn't say it aloud.

Amelia looked down at her list, pretending to busy herself with her shopping, then muttered. ''It's been *so nice* to see you, Miss Effie. But I simply must finish this shopping. Aunt Witty's waiting.''

She darted off down another aisle, pushing her cart swiftly in front of her, leaving Effie openmouthed and glaring.

''Well!'' Effie huffed. ''I know when I've been lied to.''

She made a beeline for her cart as she mulled over the fact that Tulip's librarian was less than honest. She grabbed the shopping basket and two packages of cookies, ignoring the labeling as well as the fact that she'd planned to bake, and headed for the checkout line. She had things to do and people to see.

Amelia made it through the checkout line without coming unglued. But she could feel Miss Effie's gaze boring into the back of her neck as she paid for her purchases. Without looking behind her, she grabbed her sack and made a run for the door.

A vague impression of an immovable object flashed across her vision, but she was too late to react as she barrelled out of the market and straight into a man just entering.

Everything squashed between them. Her body...his chest...and the groceries she'd just purchased. And then everything started to fall, including her glasses and his cap. She grabbed at her sack, watching in dismay as her horn-rimmed glasses fell on top of the eggs. Instead of groceries, she got her finger caught in his belt buckle.

"Damn," she mumbled, and made a dive for what was left of the sack, imagining what spilled juice would do to his boots, not to mention the skirt of her best gray dress.

Tyler saw her coming, but identification was unnecessary. Of the utmost importance was moving aside. The woman seemed bent on self-inflicted suicide at his expense and he had no intention of being the brick wall that did her in.

"Look out," he cried, and grabbed for the automatic door that was in the act of closing, anxious that she not step backward and get caught.

His hand caught in her hair as she reached for the sack sliding down his knees. The more he tried to get her loose, the more entangled he became. Before he knew it, she'd grabbed the sack and his legs at the bend of his knees. Disgusted and more than a little embarrassed, he looked down and then forgot what he'd been about to say.

Her hair! It was magnificent...and so familiar. Sunlight caught in the long, rich cascade of chestnut curls falling about her shoulders. He took a deep breath and started to kneel, intent on digging his fingers into the warm, brown heat when she looked up.

He froze in his tracks. Those eyes! He'd seen the same

bewitching shade of blue-green before. One night on a riverboat…and in his dreams…and at The Old South. Only a woman named Amber had been wearing them.

Amelia came to her senses enough to look up and then panicked. Oh my God! Tyler!

Horrified, she ducked her head and began fumbling wildly through the groceries for her glasses. When she found them, she slid them up her nose in a fit of panic. With shaking hands, she grabbed at the hair falling loose around her face and wound it up into a knot without saying a word. An inarticulate thanks was all she could manage as he retrieved her hairpins from the ground and silently handed them to her.

While Tyler watched openmouthed, Amelia began stuffing the unbroken contents of what was left of her groceries back into the sack.

She all but ran to her car. When the engine started, she peeled out of the store parking lot in a cloud of blue smoke. As she wheeled down the street, it crossed her mind that she'd possibly underestimated the Chrysler. She hadn't known there was any "peeling" left in the old crate. All she could think about was getting away from Tyler and getting home to her aunts, and safety.

Tyler stared, dumbfounded by the Beauchamp niece and her actions. Blood rushed to his head and then down to his feet. He didn't know whether to sit down or run after her. He watched Effie Dettenberg come bustling out of the grocery store and then give him a wide berth as she headed down the street.

"I'd tell myself I'm dreaming," he muttered, "but Miss Effie's never been in my dreams. Only a woman called Amber."

As he said her name aloud, he turned and stared again at the receding taillights of an old blue Chrysler, then shoved his hands into his pockets and made a small U-turn on his boot heels before he looked down the street again. A tiny smile appeared, lighting the blue of his eyes into a transparent burst of joy. It spread down across his face and sat on his lips as if it belonged.

"Well I'll be damned to hell and back. I think I just found you, sweetheart. I don't know what you're playing at, but I do believe the game is over."

He couldn't imagine what that minx of a woman was up to, but *intrigued* didn't begin to describe what he was feeling. A grin slipped right past his shock, and moments later, he began to laugh. If he wasn't crazy, and there was some talk of it because he *did* stay out in the sun too long, he'd gone and fallen in love with that old-maid niece of the Beauchamp sisters. Only the woman he'd fallen in love with was no staid, stuffy librarian. She was all fire and laughter, and sweet as sin.

Miss Effie was halfway down the block when Tyler started to laugh, but she heard it as surely as if the devilish man himself was right behind her. Her stride lengthened and her pace increased as she turned the corner, heading for home.

"What's this world coming to?" she muttered. "A woman's not safe anymore. Don't know who to trust. No sireee. You can't trust a soul these days."

When she turned the last corner toward home, she saw Maurice sitting at the edge of a thicket and licking his whiskers. She swooped him off of his feet and then gasped.

"Mouse breath! Maurice, you animal! You know what those creatures do to your indigestion."

With a groan of dismay, she clutched him fast between the sack of groceries and her flabby chest, scolding him as she went. This time, poor Maurice didn't have anyone to run interference for him. He caught hell for his indiscretions, a librarian's lie and a wild man's reputation.

Five

Tyler went through the entire day dazed from his discovery. The little witch he'd gone and fallen in love with was masquerading as a lemon-sour librarian…or vice-versa. He hadn't quite figured out which.

It had been all he could do to wait for sundown, because when the sun went down and the moon came up—when it got dark—Amber came out of hiding. At least, that was his hypothesis. He had only to make one last trip to The Old South and confront Amber with a dilemma he knew she couldn't solve, and he'd have his answer.

A blob of shaving cream fell from his razor and landed with a plop into the sink. He squinted his eyes and tilted his chin, angling for the best sweep that would take the razor across his face and his day's growth of whiskers with it.

No matter what it took, he had to look good tonight. He had to make himself so presentable, so enticing, that it would be difficult for Amber to say no. And then he grinned at himself in the mirror as he splashed himself with aftershave. But if she's who I think she is, "no" is all she can say.

He dressed with a flourish and started out to his truck, then pivoted as he remembered his gift. A bouquet of long-stemmed red roses held center stage in most of his refrigerator. He took them out, shifting the juice and milk back where they belonged while mentally berating himself for not getting a bottle of wine to go with them. And then it dawned on him that Amber could provide all the celebrating potions they needed. It was her job.

With all his bribery in place, he headed out of his driveway, turning toward Savannah at the crossroads with a smile hovering about his lips. He could hardly wait to ruin what was left of her day.

Amelia was sick with nervousness. She hadn't seen Tyler in days. At least…Amber hadn't. Ever since that morning in church when she'd had to sit through an entire sermon in the house of the Lord and face the fact that she was living a lie, she'd felt guilty. Coming out of the market today didn't count. Then she'd been Amelia and that had nearly been a disaster.

She was still counting herself lucky that he hadn't recognized her and attributed that to the fact that Aunt Rosie's prune juice had spilled all over his boots.

And she was certain she was right in assuming she'd escaped undetected. If he found her out, she had no doubt that he would have had a fit right there in the parking lot. Miss Effie would have had a field day with that.

Amelia frowned as she waited for the bartender to fill her order. She still hadn't figured out what to do about Effie Dettenberg's bombshell. Of all people to have witnessed her sneaking out of the house, she was the worst.

And today in the supermarket, Amelia had lied to Effie and she suspected Effie knew she'd been lied to. It was the silence that Effie still maintained that was making her nervous. Keeping a secret was beyond Effie.

"Girl…would you look at that?" Raelene hissed, and poked Amelia in the ribs to get her attention.

"What?" Amelia said, following Raelene's stare.

And then the man in the doorway took her breath away. He was wearing white slacks and a pale blue shirt that brought out the blue in his eyes. He was drop-dead gorgeous and carrying flowers she knew were for her. Her heart skipped a beat. Tyler!

"Go on," Raelene urged. "I'll take the drinks to your table. You go see what that 'hunk a burnin' love' wants."

Amelia grinned. Raelene had a propensity toward using outrageous phrases from time to time, and this month she was in an "Elvis Presley" frame of mind.

"Looks like I'd better take something to put out his fire."

Raelene grabbed her by the arm, cocked her painted-on eyebrows to the roof, and whispered out the side of her mouth. "Hell, no, honey. Don't put it out…fuel it. You can do it. I've seen you in action."

Thankful for the dimly lit room that hid her blush, Amelia headed for Tyler's table.

He stood as she walked up. "Evenin' darlin'," he said softly, and placed a very discreet but unforgettable kiss at the corner of her mouth.

"Evening, Tyler," she said, wishing she was anywhere but here in this outfit, with three hours to go before her shift was over.

He handed her the paper-wrapped bouquet and watched with unconcealed surprise as tears dotted the corners of her eyes. "Are you all right?" he asked sharply, suddenly imagining that she'd suffered something awful and he'd been unavailable to make it right.

"I'm fine. It's just that no one ever gave me flowers before."

"Well, they should have," he said, as he pulled her into

the shadows of the hallway leading to the dressing rooms. "But I can't say I'm sorry I'm the first. I want to be special in your eyes."

"Oh, Tyler, you already are. You can't know how much!"

Well, darlin', maybe I do, he thought. "That's great to hear," he whispered, letting his hands roam around her waist only to fasten tightly behind her back. "Move the flowers, Amber. I have a need."

Her arm dangled limply at her side, the flowers swaying against her leg as Tyler's mouth took license with her lips. Firmly yet tenderly, he started with the corners, moving across toward the middle and then on to the other side, allowing his tongue to trace the path he was taking on instinct.

Amelia shuddered, and then gasped as he centered his mouth on her mouth and himself on her. With the wall at her back, and Tyler before her she had nowhere to go but crazy. And when his tongue slipped between her lips, and his hands between their bodies, she did just that.

Tyler hadn't intended for his feelings to get so swiftly out of hand. He groaned as Amber dropped her roses and wrapped herself around him, giving back as much and more as she was getting. At that moment, he forgot his intentions and wished to be anywhere but here in a darkened hallway of The Old South.

"Hell, darlin'," he said softly, regaining some of his sanity when they came up for air. "I didn't mean for this to go so far." And then he grinned at the bewildered expression in those eyes he so loved. "Well…that's not quite truthful. I fully intend for this to go much further between us, but not right here."

Amelia blushed, then hid her face against his shirt. From the moment Tyler Dean Savage had entered The Old South, she'd lost every ounce of good sense that Wilhemina had been drumming into her head for the past twenty years.

"Have mercy, Tyler, you're driving me crazy and that's a fact."

Tyler took a deep breath. Now was the time to drop his bombshell. He almost hated to do it, because he knew when he did she was going to withdraw, and losing his hold on this woman, even temporarily, was almost more than he could bear.

Tyler gritted his teeth as he took a stand. *A man's got to do what a man's got to do. And I've got to find out if I'm going crazy, too. If you really are Amber Champion, my darlin', I'll make this up to you some day. But if you're also Amelia, I'm going to make you pay for the sleepless nights. Then and only then, can we spend them together, forever.*

He nuzzled the corner of her ear. "Amber?"

"Hmmm?" she mumbled, trying to focus on what he was saying and not what he was doing.

"I know The Old South isn't open on Sunday morning, so I got this idea."

Amelia tensed. She didn't like the sound of this.

"How about going to church with me? I want you to meet my friends—show you off a little bit. What do you say? I go to church in Tulip and I know that you'd enjoy the services. Afterwards, we could go out to my place, maybe have a picnic. I could show you my farm, and the crops, and whatever else I have you might be wanting to see."

He grinned, waiting for the last of what he'd just said to sink in. The shock on her face signaled reception of the sexual innuendo. The panic in her eyes told him the rest of his proposal was also received.

Amelia pushed herself away from the wall. "Oh Tyler, I can't. I'd truly love to. But I just can't."

He pretended to frown. "I don't see why not, unless you haven't been entirely honest with me. You said there was no one else. Maybe you were lying to me, Amber. Were you?"

The frown was fake, but Amelia was too upset to notice. She'd known something like this might happen. She just hadn't expected it to come on the heels of Effie's discovery.

Oh God, what should I do?

If she told him the truth, there was no way of guessing how he'd take the fact that he'd been tricked about her identity. Lots of men didn't like to think that could happen. Even worse, how would a sexy man like Tyler accept the fact that he'd been hornswoggled by a sexless librarian.

"No, I wasn't lying to you," she argued. "But there's still something I have to work out concerning my private life. When I do, you'll be the first to know it. Until then, you'll just have to trust me."

Tyler turned his back on Amber, trying desperately not to grin and give himself away. She was doing exactly what he'd expected. He'd been right!

Lowering his voice to imply hurt that wasn't there, he let his shoulders slump. "I don't know that I can, Amber. Trust is a two-way street. I trusted you. But you obviously don't trust me enough to explain the situation. I don't think this relationship has any place else to go."

He started to walk away. Amelia was in shock. She was about to lose the only man she'd ever loved and all because she'd lied about who she was. He'd gone and fallen in love with someone who didn't exist.

"Tyler! Wait!"

But he only shook his head and walked away. Amelia stared down at the flowers on the floor and then turned her face to the wall and wondered how long it would take to die on the spot.

Raelene poked her head around the doorway, frowning at what she saw. "Hey, are you all right?"

Amelia swiped at her tears and plastered a sickly smile on her face. She had to get through this night somehow. When she got back to Tulip, then she could cry. Now was not the time because it wasn't the ladylike thing to do.

"I'm fine," she said. And then she tilted her chin and stepped over the flowers lying on the floor.

Amelia stared at her reflection in the mirror over her vanity. She debated with the idea of leaving her hair down as she had a few days earlier. Eyes shadowed from sleepless nights stared back at her, accusing her of losing the only man she'd ever truly loved to a woman who didn't exist.

Amelia grabbed a hairbrush and began to wind her hair up into its usual topknot. "I don't get it. All I wanted was to buy a car, not ruin my life. How did this get so messed up?"

As she jabbed the last hairpin in place, she relished the pain as pin connected with too much scalp. She deserved it and more. If a miracle didn't occur, she'd already lost Tyler.

She belted her dress, turning first one way and then the other before the dressing mirror, checking the hemline for a drooping slip. There was none. Just long legs beneath a long beige skirt, and beige was not her color!

For a moment she toyed with the idea of wearing that red dress to work that she'd purchased for her date with Tyler, picturing the heart attacks that would follow. The notion quickly passed. She wasn't up to any more upheavals.

"Ahmeelya!" Wilhemina called loudly from the foot of the stairs. "Are you ready to go? You're going to be late."

Amelia rolled her eyes. It was the same thing every morning. Aunt Witty felt obligated to hurry her along when in actuality Amelia had never been late to work a day in her life.

"Coming," she called.

"Here's your lunch," Wilhemina announced, thrusting a paper sack into her niece's hands. "Don't forget to put it in the cooler when you get to the library. It's tuna fish and it would spoil."

"Yes, ma'am."

Amelia started out the door when something, either a tug of conscience or the need to be held, halted her exit. She turned.

Wilhemina gave her niece a cursory once-over. She looked presentable and unobtrusive, just the way a lady should appear. "Did you forget something?"

"Yes, ma'am." With a long, heartfelt sigh, she wrapped her arms around her aunt's bony shoulders, buried her nose in the familiar scent of rose water at the collar of Wilhemina's dress, and hugged.

Wilhemina was in shock. She'd couldn't remember when her niece had been so demonstrative. "Why Amelia! There, there," she said, awkwardly patting Amelia's back. "Go on with you girl," she said, masking her emotion with a swift sniff.

Amelia sighed again as she headed out the door.

"I'm making apple dumplings tonight," Wilhemina called out. She hadn't intended to. The thought had come about the same time Amelia had hugged her.

Amelia paused and then smiled. "Good. I'll save room for two."

Rosemary dawdled out of the flower garden and onto the porch just as Amelia was driving away. The wilting bouquet of bachelor buttons she'd cut hung precariously from a basket filled with everything from the weeds she'd pulled to a terrapin she'd fished from the azalea bed.

She dropped wearily into the wicker chair beneath the veranda's welcome shade. "I heard you through the open window, Sister. You only make apple dumplings on special occasions."

Wilhemina's mouth pursed, unwilling to admit that the reason she'd said what she had was from love, not duty. "So?"

Rosemary fiddled with her hat and dropped it and the basket with its interesting contents beside her chair. "So, did I forget someone's birthday?'' Her eyes lit up. ''It's not already Independence Day, is it?''

''Rosemary!'' Wilhemina's sharp voice changed the route of their conversation. Both forgot what they'd been talking about as the terrapin waddled its way out of the shallow basket. ''There's a terrapin in your basket!''

Rosemary rolled her eyes. ''I know that. I put it in there. Sometimes I think you don't give me credit for anything, Willy.''

Wilhemina frowned. ''Sister, why would you put a terrapin in the flower basket?''

''Where else would I put it?'' she asked, astonished that Willy had to even ask. ''My pocket is too small, of course.''

''Of course,'' Wilhemina muttered. ''Why didn't I think of that?''

Rosemary smiled. It was an angelic smile that lit up her face and took years off her eighty-something countenance. She patted her sister's wrinkled hand and leaned back in the chair, relishing the breeze that had just sprung up.

''It's all right, Willy, dear. That's why you have me.''

Tyler's eyes narrowed as he watched Amelia park the family Chrysler beneath the twin magnolias beside Cuspus Albert Marquiside's marker. The stiff breeze that had blown up only minutes before quickly plastered the skirt of her dress against those long, shapely legs. He smiled to himself, thankful that he was the only male in Tulip who knew what charms lay beneath that colorless exterior.

He'd been waiting forty-five minutes for the library to open. Never having frequented the establishment, he'd been unaware of their business hours, but he had a need to visit Miss Amelia Ann and make use of her knowledge as Tulip's librarian. He fully intended to get under her skin just as deftly as he'd perturbed Amber. And he knew just how to do it.

Sighing in appreciation for the way the wind had outlined that marvelous figure for his eyes only, he watched her unlock the library door and slip inside, then he waited. When he went in, he intended to be the only customer. To his relief, no one came, and when she turned the Closed sign to Open, he made his move.

Amelia was changing the due date on the stamp she used to mark books when Tyler walked in. She closed the lid on the stamp pad and swallowed twice in rapid succession. In all the years she'd worked as librarian, Tyler Savage had never once visited the library. Her mind raced at the implications of his appearance this morning.

"Morning, Miss Amelia," he said softly.

"Mr. Savage."

Her greeting was short and succinct. She was still very angry with him for walking out on her last night at The Old South, although to be fair, it wasn't actually Amelia he'd left standing, it had been Amber.

He smiled slowly, then leaned forward until he was nearly nose to nose with her shocked expression.

Amelia was so surprised by his unexpected behavior she forgot to move. When she realized she could feel his breath against her lips, she jerked back in confusion and shifted her glasses to a more comfortable position across her nose.

"Was there something I could do for you?" she asked, and hated him when his blue eyes sparkled. The cad! He was reading something into her offer other than what she'd intended to imply.

He straightened up. "You could say that."

In spite of it all, she was just the least bit pleased that he was going to get a glimpse of her in action doing the job for which she'd trained. She held her hand poised above the old-fashioned card catalog, ready to search out the volumes he would request. "That's just fine. How may I be of service?"

"It's like this…last night I couldn't sleep."

Shock spread across her face.

"And so I watched a late-night show on television that I don't normally watch."

This was getting her nowhere. "Yes?"

"They mentioned a book that I thought sounded interesting. One I think would probably be well worth my time to read."

Amelia was surprised. Tyler was a lot of things, but a bookworm she would not have suspected. "That's fine, Tyler," she said. "What was the title?" Her fingers remained poised above the cards.

He stared up at the ceiling, as if trying to remember. "Ummm, I think it had something to do with sex."

Amelia tried not to stutter and dared not stare. "Excuse me?"

"Now I remember! I think the book was called *The Joy of Sex.* It sounded really interesting. Ever read it?"

Tyler was enjoying the shock and reluctant intrigue that kept appearing and disappearing in those beautiful blue-green eyes. Even behind those old-fashioned glasses he could see her distress—and her interest.

"I can't say that I have," she mumbled, and began searching the card catalog for the title, although she'd bet every penny she'd ever made at The Old South that it wasn't on the shelves of Tulip Public Library. Effie Dettenberg was on the library board and there was no way anything like that would ever have passed her approval.

Amelia shuffled cards, her fingers trembling as she tried not to shriek at him for what he'd done to her last night. And then she nearly fainted when his hand slid forward and gently brushed across her hair. She jerked and looked up in shock.

"You had a bit of leaf in your hair," he explained.

To Amelia's dismay, he winked. She glared. How dare he flirt with someone else when her back—that is, Amber's back—was turned? Just look what he was capable of!

He leaned forward, his voice just above a whisper. "So...have you ever had it here?"

Amelia had lost her train of thought and had even for-gotten for a moment why he was here.

"Had what?" she muttered.

"You know…*The Joy of Sex.*"

She blushed furiously. He was implying a hell of a lot more than reading material and they both knew it. With a tilt of her chin, she began to search the place in the card catalog where her fingers had stopped, and then looked down, trying to figure out why she was in the *Xs*. She sighed with dismay. *Where else would I be? My feelings for Tyler Savage are strictly X-rated.*

"All we have on the subject is back here," she mut-tered. "Follow me."

Gladly, my darling.

As Amelia turned away, Tyler made a quick dash to the front door. Before she knew that he'd moved, he'd turned the lock and the Open sign to Closed.

"Back here," she called.

"I'm coming." He followed her through the stacks.

She had two separate books in her hand when he walked up behind her and then nearly dropped them both as he pinned her between his body and the shelves.

His quick breath feathered the wisps of hair dangling down the back of her neck. She closed her eyes, shudder-ing with longing as his fingers traced up and down in the space between her hair and collar.

"Warm back here, isn't it, Amelia?"

"What do you think you're doing?" It was a stupid question. She knew full well what he was doing. She just wasn't certain what she was going to do about it.

"Your skin is so soft," he whispered. "Does it taste as good as it looks?"

She whirled around in panic, unwilling for him to test his theory.

"Tyler Savage!"

It was all she could say. He'd ignored her existence for her entire life and now this? It was a puzzle she couldn't decipher. And what was worse, she had liked what was happening. She was letting this two-timing cur have his way with her.

"How dare you be so familiar?" she hissed. "We've hardly ever spoken."

With a sigh, he reached up and pulled a single hairpin from her topknot. "I know, but it's hardly all my fault. You won't even look at me when we meet on the street."

"Even so," she mumbled, and tried to push past him.

He stepped to one side, blocking her retreat with little effort as the hairpin fell to the floor. Then he cupped her face in his hands and leaned down. His nose bumped on the edge of her glasses and a soft, unintelligible curse slipped from his lips as he lifted them from her face and placed them on the shelf behind her.

Amelia was in panic. He was taking her apart at the seams and when he was finished, she would have no defenses behind which to hide. "Stop this, right now," she whispered. "You have no..."

The word "right" would have finished her sentence. But when his mouth closed over her lips, pressing gently and persistently, "right" was the only thing that came to mind. Loving this man was right. Holding this man was right. Amelia was in love and had been for so long right was all that mattered. And then she remembered. Where did this leave Amber?

"Amelia?" Tyler's soft question slipped out between their lips.

She staggered as he released her. "What?"

"Would you do me the honor of going out to dinner with me tonight? I'd like very much to get to know you better. Maybe if you'd give me a chance, you could learn to care for me. What do you think?"

Oh no! I have to work tonight! This is getting to be a comedy of horrors! I can't go out with him as Amber, and now I can't go out with him as Amelia, either! Life is not fair!

Trying to kill time while searching for a reasonable answer, she bent down to retrieve her hairpin. "I can't. I have to...I mean I've already promised to..."

She shoved her glasses back up her nose and tried not to remember how it felt to be held in his arms.

He pretended to wilt. "Never mind. I understand. You don't trust me, and I suppose it's my fault. But I swear that my reputation is based on unfounded rumors. Truth got lost somewhere in the telling, I promise."

Amelia tried to be angry. It was only last night that he'd held her...*held Amber*...and begged for something entirely different. What was with this man? She couldn't trust him. He was two-timing them both.

"I thought you had a girlfriend in Savannah," she accused, and then gulped nervously as a strange, dark gleam appeared in his eyes. She would have sworn his mouth twitched, but she could have been mistaken.

"I thought I did, too," he said softly. "But she obviously didn't want anything to do with me. I guess we weren't right for each other. I obviously wasn't her kind of man."

"That's not true!" Amelia shouted, and then nearly fainted at what she'd almost revealed. "I mean...well, I don't know what I mean, but I can't go out with you tonight and that's that. Do you want these books or not?" She shoved them beneath his nose.

Tyler was fighting his instincts. They told him to simply swing her up in his arms and demand an explanation. But there was obviously more to this woman than pure beauty. She was loaded with brains—and a fair amount of deceit. It was an intriguing combination he had no intention of losing.

"I guess not," he said, and headed for the door. "I don't really know what I want, Amelia. It's obvious that the women I seem to be attracted to don't feel the same way toward me. Maybe I should just call it quits."

She was dumbstruck. If she read him right, and she was

desperately afraid that she had, he'd just dumped both her and Amber.

"Just because I can't go tonight doesn't mean I never could," Amelia said suddenly.

Tyler stopped but he didn't turn around. He didn't dare. The smile on his face was too wide and too knowing. He managed to nod, as if giving her statement its due consideration, and then turned the lock on the door.

"That's good," he said quietly. "Maybe if I get up enough nerve to face being turned down again, I'll give you a call. Have a nice day, Amelia."

He turned the Closed sign to Open and walked out the door, taking care not to let it slam, then drove like a bat out of hell until he was three miles outside Tulip's city limits. He stopped and got out of his pickup truck and started to grin. The more he thought about it, the funnier it got. He didn't know why, and he didn't know how, but as God was his witness, he was going to marry those women if it killed him. The thought was so incongruous that he began to laugh aloud, slapping his knee and then leaning against the side of his truck to catch his breath.

A short time later a neighbor came driving by and started to stop, thinking that he'd broken down. He waved them on as he crawled back in his truck and headed for home. Loving a woman like that just *might* kill him. And then he grinned. But what a way to go!

Six

Amelia was running, but for once, not down an alley. She was through with deceit. Wearing a sweatsuit, tennis shoes and a determined look that Wilhemina would have called defiant, she ran toward the corner where Raelene Stringer was waiting.

Effie Dettenberg stood at her front window, peeking through the lace curtains. To her amazement, Amelia waved as she jogged past the house. Effie dropped the curtains back in place, disgusted at being caught spying.

"She doesn't fool me," Effie muttered, and headed for the upstairs window with her new binoculars in hand. She was going to see for herself just what Amelia Beauchamp was up to, certain it would be to no good. Maurice wound himself around her ankles, slowing her ascent, but not her determination.

"Get," she scolded, and frowned as he hissed and then sauntered away.

Amelia's heart was pounding. She felt as if she'd run a

mile when it had only been around the corner. But it wasn't because she was winded. She was exhilarated. She'd made a decision about her life that was long overdue. Now all she had to do was tell Raelene the news.

"You're early," Raelene said, as Amelia jogged up.

"I'm not going," she said shortly. "I've made a decision. Would you tell the boss that I quit, or moved, or died. Something…anything, I don't care which. I just can't go back there again. Okay?"

She hated to let Raelene down when she'd been such a good friend, but she'd reached the limit of her endurance with regards to deceit. Raelene had kept Amelia's secret like a true friend and she felt she owed her some sort of explanation.

Raelene crawled out of her car with a grin on her face. "I've been expecting this, honey. Is it about to hit the fan?"

Amelia shrugged. "I don't think so, but I think it's time I stopped before it does."

"Shoot! Anything's okay with me. You ought to know that by now."

Amelia threw her arms around Raelene's neck, ignoring the fact that they were standing in plain sight of anyone who chose to drive down the street.

"I can't thank you enough," Amelia said, her voice shaking as tears threatened. "And I think I'm going to miss driving to work with you, even if I don't miss the job. You've been a true friend to me."

"Well, hell, honey," Raelene sniffed. "I'll miss you, too. But you better get on back before someone else misses you."

Amelia shrugged, knowing she was referring to her aunts. "They're already asleep. But you're right. I'd better get back. It's almost dark, and you know what they say. A lady isn't safe out after dark."

They looked at each other and then burst out laughing, remembering the countless hours they'd shared in the dark-

ened club and then driving back to Tulip alone in Raelene's old car.

"Well now, I'd better hurry or I'm gonna be late," Raelene said, and got back in her car.

Amelia waved and then winced as Raelene ground the
gears. The car belched once for good measure and then
popped and hopped its way out of Tulip.

Amelia watched until the taillights of the car had disappeared, then turned toward home. For the first time in
months she was going to get to bed before 2:00 a.m. One
secret was over, but she was still filled with regret over
the loss of Tyler.

Thinking about him made tears come to her eyes. She
could just see Tyler coming into The Old South in search
of Amber and then leaving with no idea of how to ever
find her. Amelia wanted Tyler with every ounce of her
being, but he wanted Amber. For all intents and purposes,
she no longer existed.

Her footsteps dragged. Yes, he had flirted with Amelia,
but she didn't believe he'd meant it. She'd come to the
conclusion that he'd done it just to prove to himself he
was still desirable after Amber had turned him down. She
sighed. What must he be feeling now when even the old-
maid librarian of Tulip, Georgia had told him "no"?

She kicked at a rock on the sidewalk and sniffed. He
couldn't be half as miserable as she felt. The only thing
she'd gained out of this entire mess was enough money to
finally buy her car. However, it wasn't nearly as attractive
a thought as it once had been. It faded perceptibly in her
mind. A big man with dark hair and blue eyes and a smile
that could start fires kept getting in the way.

A short time later, she walked back into the house and
closed and locked the door. Amelia Ann was home for
good.

Across the street, Miss Effie set her binoculars down
onto the table with a thump.

"Well, I saw it for myself," she muttered. "She actually

hugged that…that woman…in broad daylight. They were
giggling and laughing as if they were bosom buddies. But
I wonder why she didn't go? I wonder…"

Maurice howled loudly downstairs, begging to be put
out.

"Coming, dear," Effie called. For the moment Amelia's
business was set aside as Maurice's needs were met.

Tyler ached. In every joint. In every muscle. He'd
worked himself to the point of exhaustion three days running just so that he could sleep at night and then defeated
his own purpose by dreaming about the same woman he
was desperately trying to avoid.

But he had a plan. He knew Amber had quit work at
the club because he'd made a point of calling to find out.
Now all that remained was to give Amelia time to digest
the fact that Tyler would no longer be seeing Amber, therefore leaving Amelia an open field. At least he hoped Amelia saw it that way. It was all that kept him going.

He stared out across the fields, green and rich from the
abundant crops growing beneath the ground. It was nearly
dark. Time to call it a day. Reluctantly, he turned back
toward his house, but the thought of going inside alone
was almost more than he could bear. Tonight maybe he'd
allow himself one concession to the plan. Maybe…just
maybe…he would make a phone call. And maybe…just
maybe…after he heard her voice, he'd know whether or
not his plan was working.

"You seem sad, dear," Rosemary remarked, as they
finished the evening meal. "Are you well?"

Amelia jerked into an upright position, realizing that
she'd been as slumped as her spirits, and made herself
smile.

"Of course I'm well, Aunt Rosie, but you're a dear for
asking. Here, have some more pie. Aunt Witty outdid her-

self tonight, don't you think? Custard was always one of her specialties.''

Rosemary nodded and accepted another tiny sliver of the delectable dessert. Wilhemina stared pointedly at her sister's second helping and then even more sharply at her niece.

Amelia was rambling and she knew it. She just hoped the aunts didn't catch onto the fact. It was fairly easy to put Rosemary off the track. In fact, her aunt Rosie's track was often off course. But Aunt Witty was another matter altogether. She didn't live in the past and daydreams. She had both feet planted firmly in the present, and if anything, was more astute with each passing year.

''I noticed you're wearing your hair down again,'' Wilhemina said. ''Are you having more of your headaches?''

Amelia wanted to cry. Headaches were only the beginning. Her heart hurt in so many places it was a wonder it still beat. She missed seeing Tyler. She missed hearing his voice and seeing that teasing smile. And most of all she missed being held. And it was all her own fault.

She sighed and finally answered. ''Not really, Aunt Witty. I just felt like a change. In fact, I think change is good for the soul every now and then, don't you?''

Rosemary brightened considerably as her sister's frown increased.

''Oh, I do,'' Rosemary chirped. ''Don't you, Sister? Remember when Momma wanted to change the rug in the parlor and Poppa had a fit about the colors. Wasn't that the funniest thing? They didn't speak for weeks and it was all because you mentioned that the pink in the flowers was the same color as the bald spot on the top of his head.''

Wilhemina rolled her eyes and tried not to smile. It *had* been humorous. ''Yes, well, I was only five or six, but it was an unintentional slight that Poppa never got over.''

''That's because his bald spot kept getting bigger,'' Rosemary said.

Amelia laughed. No matter what else she'd lost, she still

had her precious family and she'd die before she'd lose them, too.

And then the phone rang.

Silence reigned. Everyone stared at the other as shock spread into the room. No one ever called them after dark! In fact, it was rare that they received a call at all.

Rosemary couldn't have been more excited if General Lee had just announced himself at the front door. "It's the phone!"

"I know it's the phone," Wilhemina muttered. "But who could be calling at this hour?"

Amelia was in shock. She couldn't remember the last time the phone had rung. "It's just seven-thirty, Aunt Witty. And there's only one way to find out. I'll get it!"

"No, you don't," Wilhemina ordered, and headed for the table in the hall. "I'll do it. And I'll give whoever it is a piece of my mind for calling so late, too."

Rosemary looked crestfallen. If her sister yelled at them they'd never call back. And having a phone call at night seemed so sociable. Rosemary liked socials. She wished they'd come back in style.

"Hello!" Wilhemina's greeting was full of accusation, but her disgust turned to dismay as she listened to the man and his request. She turned and stared at Amelia as if she'd just grown horns. "It's for you. It's that Tyler Savage!"

"Oh, goody," Rosemary gushed. "I just love that boy. He reminds me of…"

Amelia was dumbstruck. She took the phone from her aunt's hands and then tried not to smile as Tyler's deep, familiar voice reverberated in her eardrum.

"Hello?"

Tyler smiled, then relaxed. At least she'd come to the phone. That meant she was still willing to talk. He stretched his long body across the bed and held the phone just the least bit closer to his mouth. If he couldn't have Amelia here in bed with him, the least he could do was lie in the damned bed when he talked to her. It was better than the silence with which he'd been living.

"How have you been?" he asked.

"Fine, I guess."

He heard more than what she intended for him to hear. He recognized the pain and longing in her voice. He should, it was an echo of his own feelings.

"Have you given any more thought to what I asked you the other day? About going out with me sometime?"

Amelia almost giggled with joy. He'd been serious! She wanted to cry. She wanted to laugh. But she couldn't do anything but maintain a ladylike image because Aunt Witty was breathing down her neck.

"Some," she said softly. "In fact, I have a problem that I think you might be able to help me with."

He closed his eyes and groaned as his fingers clenched around the receiver. He had a problem, too, and it hurt like hell. Making love to Amelia for the next fifty years would just about solve his problem if she'd only...

"I'd be glad to help you in any way I can," he said. "When can we meet to talk about your problems?"

"How about Saturday? That is, if you're not busy."

Honey, I'd plow under a whole damn crop if that's what it took to see you. "That would be fine with me," he said.

"Good. Then I'll meet you...."

"No! I'll come to *your* house. I'll pick *you* up. You're not meeting me anywhere, okay?"

In that moment, something familiar rang a bell, but she lost her train of thought when Wilhemina gasped and Rosemary clapped her hands in delight.

"Okay," she said. "And thanks for calling."

Thank you, lady, Tyler thought, and smiled as she disconnected.

"Just what is the meaning of this?" Wilhemina asked.

"Meaning of what, Aunt Witty?"

"Seeing a man like that? And don't play innocent with me, missy. You know what I mean. Why did he call you?

Have you been seeing him behind my back?'' Wilhemina was full of indignation.

''For pity's sake, Willy. She's twenty-nine years old. She can see anyone she chooses, whether it's behind your back or behind the barn.'' Rosemary giggled at her own wit. ''And I can't see anything wrong with that boy. After all, his own mother was one of your friends in school.''

Wilhemina sniffed. ''But he has a terrible reputation. Why, I remember when…''

''Pooh,'' Rosemary said. ''That was years ago. I'm sure he's gentled. And besides, a man's not a man unless he's sown a few wild oats. Remember when Poppa got caught…''

Wilhemina didn't want to hear that old story again. Momma had threatened to go back to New Orleans when it had happened. It had taken every ounce of persuasion her father'd had to stop her. Her voice got shrill.

''I don't know why you can't remember where you put your purse yesterday and you can remember everything that happened nearly seventy years ago. It makes no sense. No sense at all.''

''Yes it does,'' Rosemary said. And for once, the poignancy of her answer silenced them all. ''I remember the early years because they were the best. Nothing happened to us later except that we got old, Willy. Nothing happened—nothing at all.''

''One thing happened,'' Amelia said. ''You got me.''

The sisters stared at each other and then shared a rare smile. ''That's true,'' they echoed. ''We got you.''

For the time being Tyler's call was forgotten. It was only later, when Wilhemina had started to drift off to sleep that she remembered it. And then it was too late to do anything about it. But there was always tomorrow. She'd deal with it then.

''He's here!'' Rosemary called, and then yanked open the front door before Tyler had a chance to knock.

"Good morning, Tyler Dean," Rosemary said. "Do come in. Amelia will be right down."

Tyler tried not to grin, but it was hopeless. Rosemary Beauchamp was wearing the most enchanting little smile. It went well with her pink organza dress and her tennis shoes.

"Been out for a walk?"

"Oh yes," she said. "It's quite healthy, you know."

"Yes, ma'am," Tyler said. "I do a bit of it myself."

She beamed, pleased that they had so much in common. Pleased that he had such dark hair and flashing eyes. Pleased that there was a man in the house. It didn't take much to please Rosemary, but Wilhemina wasn't cut from the same cloth. There was little that satisfied her.

He watched as the elder sister entered the room and wondered how he would ever find common ground with her.

"Miss Wilhemina, it's real good to see you again."

She nodded. "Please, have a seat, Amelia should be here soon."

"After you, ma'am," he said, and quietly stood beside a chair until Wilhemina had taken a seat.

Wilhemina sat, judging his behavior and finding no fault. Well, he has manners, I'll give him that, she thought. It's been years since I've seen any man who knew the right way to treat a lady. Everyone knows a gentleman doesn't seat himself until every woman in the room is sitting down.

Of course, if Wilhemina had been honest with herself, she would have had to admit that she hadn't been around a man—any man—in so many years that it hardly counted.

"Just what is your business here?" she asked.

Tyler tried not to flinch. He wondered how long it would take her to haul out the gun if he told her the truth. It wouldn't do to admit he wanted to bed her niece in the world's worst way. What the hell could he say that wouldn't get him in trouble? As he was searching for an answer, Amelia walked into the room.

"Why, Amelia, don't you look pretty!"

Rosemary's statement was echoed by Tyler but it was hardly as eloquent. His sounded more like a grunt. And that was because he felt like he'd just been kicked in the stomach. Muscles he hadn't used in months came alive, including some that had no business doing so. He took a deep breath, closed his eyes and counted to ten, then added another five for good measure before he opened them and tried not to stare.

She had on a new dress. It *was* a shirtwaist. But it was sleeveless…and shorter than usual…and the most beautiful shade of peach he'd ever seen. The tight, ugly knot she normally made of her hair was gone. It was hanging loose and tied at the back of her neck with a slip of matching peach ribbon. Tiny wisps of baby-size curls fluffed around her face, framing it to perfection.

She hadn't had the nerve to wear her contacts. It would have been the end of their beginning if he'd recognized her as Amber. So, the owl-rimmed glasses hung precariously on the bridge of her nose just as they did every day at the library. She was still Amelia, but she'd let just the least little bit of Amber shine through.

Wilhemina tried not to fidget. She didn't like this new turn of events. In fact, she didn't like anything new. If it had been good enough for Poppa, it was still good enough for her. Trusting men would constitute a change. She would have none of it.

"Where do you plan to go?" she asked sharply.

Amelia leaned over and kissed her aunts on their cheeks.

"It's a surprise," she said. "When I come back, then you'll see."

Tyler was just as mystified as the aunts. He didn't know what Amelia had in mind, and quite frankly didn't give a damn. As long as he could spend the day with this woman, he'd give just about anything a try.

"I'm ready," she announced.

Tyler jumped to his feet, waved goodbye to the two

elderly women and tried not to sweat as he watched Amelia's hips swaying gently from side to side as she walked down the front porch steps ahead of him.

"Where are you taking me, Amelia?" he asked, trying to tease that serious expression from her face. Her answer couldn't have come as more of a shock if she'd asked him to bed Miss Effie just as a personal favor.

"I have need of your services, Tyler."

Ooh, darlin', I have need of yours, too. "I'm at your disposal."

"Good! Then take me to Savannah. I want to buy a car."

Hiding his relief at the news, he nodded solemnly, seated her in the truck, and then slid behind the wheel, trying not to laugh from the joy. The reason for the extra job! She hadn't been working there because she wanted to meet men. It hadn't been because she liked the nightlife and flashy clothes. She wanted to buy a car! And then another thought occurred, one that wasn't so cheerful.

The dark, brooding look he gave her was unintentional. But his reason for concern soon became evident.

"I'd be most happy to help," he said quietly. "At least, I would if you're not planning to leave Tulip just as soon as you get it."

"Oh, my no! I just want to be able to travel around a little before I'm too old to see what's out there. I have no intention of going anywhere. I wouldn't leave my aunts, or Tulip." She blushed and paused. "Or anyone else, not for all the cars and money in the world."

Tyler smiled. He'd never wanted to kiss anyone this desperately in his entire life. He was pinning all his hopes on her "or anyone else." He had to be the "else." It was all that got him through a day.

"Okay then, did you have a particular model picked out, or are you flexible?"

"Whatever $12,000 dollars will buy, and as long as it's a fairly late model and red. I like red."

He grinned. Red! She was just full of surprises.

"Red it is, darlin'. Now hang on. We've got to spend your money before the sun goes down."

She caught his excitement and patted her purse to make sure her checkbook was inside. This day had been long in coming in more ways than one.

She snuck a quick peek at the man behind the wheel. There was one thing a woman could want from a man like that and it had nothing to do with money and red cars. She blushed just thinking about it and quickly stared out the window.

But Tyler had seen her look, and before she knew what had happened, he'd pulled her next to him. So close that when he shifted gears or applied the brake, their thighs brushed. She swallowed once and tried not to look down at the length of long, strong leg encased in denim, but it was no use. There was simply too much of him to ignore. And, she wondered, as they entered the outskirts of Savannah, why a woman would even want to try.

"You're sure this is the one you want?" Tyler asked. They'd taken it out for the third test run and each time, he'd watched the smile in her eyes grow brighter.

"Oh yes! It's small, economical and four-door so that my aunts can get in and out with ease, and best of all, it's red!"

Tyler grinned. She was right on that count. It was truly the reddest car he'd seen in years. The salesman called it fire-engine red. He called it hell on wheels.

"Okay, then let me deal. I think I can get him to lower the price some more. It'll save you at least a thousand. You can use what you save for the tax and title change. Wait here. I'll see what I can do."

She nodded and plopped down on the bench inside the dealership, trying not to let on how much she wanted the car. Tyler had already told her that if she appeared too eager, they might not come down on the price. She watched him walk away and tried not to think of how much she wanted the man. If she did, they'd know she wanted *something* bad. They just wouldn't know it was the man, not the car, that had her all hot and bothered.

He was back before she had time to think about how she was going to tell her aunts.

"Okay, sweetheart. You've just bought yourself a car. Write him a check for $10,200.00 and let's take her home."

Amelia jumped to her feet and before she thought, had flung herself into his arms.

"Oh, Tyler. Thank you! Thank you! I could never have done it without you."

He caught her in midflight and knew before she was through talking what he was going to do. Her mouth was slightly open. The last words had just slipped through. Her breath was short and light, peppermint-flavored from a mint he'd never seen her chew. His fingers threaded through the long length of hair caught at the back of her neck and tightened as he tasted Amelia Ann.

His mouth was firm and wide, engulfing, entreating. It coaxed and coerced until what good sense she had disappeared.

"Oh, Tyler." She sighed as he reluctantly pulled back. She looked up through misty lenses to see him watching her. To her dismay, he lifted her glasses from her nose.

"Is that all you can say?" he teased.

"Give them to me," she said quickly, grabbing her eyeglasses from his hands. She shoved them back on her nose. "I've got plenty to say, but now's not the time or place."

He grinned and watched her disappear behind those owlish rims. He did want this woman so. He just wasn't real sure who was the real Amelia Ann and who was the imposter.

Effie Dettenberg was the first to see it coming down the street, but on her way to the window to gawk, she accidentally stepped on Maurice's tail. He let out a wail and made for the stairs. Lost between the urge to console her one and only against the need to snoop, snooping won out.

She parted the lace panels and looked out as the little red compact wheeled into the driveway of the Beauchamp house, and then gasped as Amelia actually had the nerve to honk the horn.

Effie saw the aunts come out of the house, then witnessed the surprise on their faces. It was nothing to what they'd feel if they knew what she knew.

Now everything was suddenly clear. Amelia had herself a flashy new car and Effie knew good and well how she'd earned the money to get it. Why, she'd seen her consorting with Raelene Stringer with her own eyes. And everyone knew how Raelene made her money. Everyone knew that Raelene liked men—too much for her own good. It was scandalous that poor Wilhemina and poor Rosemary were so duped by that deceitful niece.

Effie sniffed and dropped the curtains. It was her duty to let them know. She just hadn't quite decided how to go about it. But she knew what she had to do. Effie was big on duties.

Seven

Amelia held her breath as the aunts came down the porch steps. Rosemary's smile of delight was expected, as was Wilhemina's frown. She got out of the car with trepidation.

"What is the meaning of this?" Wilhemina asked.

"It's my surprise," Amelia said. "I've been saving money for a long time now. It's all bought and paid for. I don't owe anyone a penny and it'll be very economical on gas."

"The Chrysler got good mileage," Wilhemina muttered.

Rosemary was entranced. She'd always wanted something red. "That's because it never got out of Tulip," she argued.

Wilhemina had been fraught with nerves at the idea of losing Amelia and uneasy about Tyler's appearance into their lives, but the appearance of the car settled part of her fears.

"So this is why you needed that man's assistance."

Amelia nodded. "It's part of it, Aunt Witty. But I like

him, as a friend. He's a very kind and generous-hearted man.''

"Pooh!" It was all Wilhemina could manage. This had been a big day in their lives. For the first time in her life, Amelia had left home with a man. And now she'd come back in a new red car. Witty didn't like upheavals.

"I think he's handsome," Rosemary announced. "And I want a ride. Can we go for a ride, Amelia? I get the front seat. After all, remember I suffer from motion sickness.''

"You don't suffer from any such thing," Wilhemina argued.

"But, Sister, I do. Remember when I got sick and threw up all over…''

"You'd just eaten three brownies and a bowl of ice cream at the church picnic, that's why you got sick—not from riding in a car.''

Amelia stopped the argument before it went further. "Both of you get in. Aunt Rosie can ride in the front this time. Next time it'll be Aunt Witty's turn.''

It stopped the fuss as they settled inside.

Tyler watched from the corner. The smile on his face spread wider as he saw Amelia slowly but surely win Wilhemina over. As the two elderly women took their seats inside the new car, he shifted gears and drove away. Yet no matter how far he drove, he couldn't get the memory of Amelia's lips off his mind.

He shivered and ran his fingers through his hair, ruffling it even more. He hoped to God he survived this woman, because if he did, she'd be worth the years off his life that loving her was probably going to take.

Miss Effie watched them load into the car and back out of the driveway. With a sniff of disdain, she changed her shoes, grabbed her handbag, and headed for the door with somebody else's business on her mind.

* * *

Amelia put a box of raisins in her shopping cart and tried to ignore the smirk the box boy gave her as he continued to stock the grocery shelves. It was not the first time she'd experienced such behavior. And it had all started five days ago when she'd come home in her new car.

Ever since then she'd been getting these strange glances. At the gas station, the grocery store, even in the library she heard whispers that stopped when she got close, and received knowing smiles from men who'd never before given her the time of day.

She had a feeling that things were only going to get worse. And she knew just who to thank for the rumors that must be floating around Tulip about her. There was only one person other than Raelene who'd seen her out late at night. Miss Effie! And there was *no* other person in Tulip who had as loose a jaw.

She sighed, ignored the soft whistle that accompanied the boy's smirk, and pushed her cart toward the checkout stand. Surely this would pass. She hadn't done anything wrong. If the library board hadn't been so stingy with her salary she would never have had to take the second job to begin with.

"Will that be all?" the clerk asked, and gave Amelia the once-over. She'd heard all about how this prissy librarian had raised the money for that flashy new car. Personally, she had a hard time believing that any man would pay good money to take out someone who looked like her. But it was true that men were fools. She guessed that they'd do a lot for their own pleasures.

Amelia nodded and reached for her purse. The young man sacked her groceries, carried them out to the car, and gave her a pat on the behind as he walked away. Amelia was so shocked she didn't know whether to slap him or run. She did neither. Instead she sank behind the wheel of her car, rested her forehead on the steering wheel and fought back tears. Something as innocent as wanting a new car had turned into a nightmare.

Effie smiled snidely as she peered into Amelia's car. She'd seen the girl lay her head on the steering wheel. It served her right. If she stayed inside at night like any decent woman, she wouldn't be tired. Burning candles at both ends simply used them up faster and left them no place on which to rest.

"Late night again?"

Amelia gritted her teeth and blinked tears. "Actually, no. I just have a headache. I seem to have a lot of them nowadays. I think it's something in the air."

She started her car and drove away, leaving Effie to take what she'd said any way she chose. She was past caring about pretense any longer. And there were two people who deserved to know the truth before these rumors reached their ears.

She carried the groceries inside the house and went in search of her aunts. She found them in the living room squabbling over a game show. Ordinarily it would have made her smile. Today, however, she feared that when she was finished, they'd be squabbling over whether or not to throw her out of the house.

When she stepped in front of the television and turned it off, their fuss ceased instantly. Amelia's pale face and strange behavior got their undivided attention.

Wilhemina was the first to speak. "What's wrong, dear?"

"Are you ill?" Rosemary asked.

Amelia shook her head, sank down into the chair beside them and burst into tears.

Wilhemina was frightened. In all the years they'd had Amelia, she'd never behaved in such a manner. It had to be Tyler Savage's fault. "It's that man! I knew this would come to no good!"

Amelia's sobs only got louder.

Suddenly, Rosemary took control. She could tell that Willy was only going to assess blame, not what had caused the damage. She scooted into the chair beside Amelia, wrapped her arms around her niece's shaking shoulders, and patted her lovingly.

"What's wrong, darling?" she asked. "You can tell us. You can tell us anything. We love you."

It was the single worst thing they could have said to her. It only added to the guilt with which she'd been living since she'd started her life of deceit. Amelia sniffed loudly, took the handkerchief Aunt Rosie offered and blew.

"It's all my fault," she said. "But I didn't mean for it to go this far, and I never intended to lie to you. I just wanted to earn some extra money for the car."

Wilhemina and Rosemary stared at each other. She was making no sense.

"Go ahead, dear," Rosemary said. "We're listening."

Amelia started talking. Wilhemina's face blanched and then turned a deep shade of rose. Rosemary's eyes widened, her mouth pursed and then a slow smile of delight deepened the wrinkled creases in her cheeks as she absorbed her niece's story.

"You mean you worked in a drinking establishment and got to wear one of those cute little outfits?"

Wilhemina glared at her sister. Sometimes she completely missed the point at hand.

"It doesn't matter what she wore," Wilhemina argued. "We both know Amelia would never do anything to shame herself or us. The point is, someone has made more of this than they should. Someone has obviously embellished upon the fact that Amelia chose to ride back and forth to her job with a woman whose reputation has, shall we say, suffered over the years for lack of guidance. However, that should in no way make Amelia part of the same cut of cloth."

Amelia threw her arms around her aunts. "I should have known you would understand. And I never actually meant to lie to you. I was going to tell you right off. But I didn't, and the longer I waited, the harder it became. And I never meant to work there forever. It was only until I'd saved enough for the car.''

Rosemary made a fist with her hands and tucked them daintily into her lap. Backbone straight, eyes gleaming, intrigue flowing from every word, she leaned forward and whispered.

''Did you *really* make all that money in wages and tips?''

Amelia nodded.

''Well I think that's just wonderful! Do you think they'd have a place for me?''

''Rosemary!'' Wilhemina's shocked response reverberated throughout the parlor.

''We could use a little extra money.'' She glared at her sister, her bottom lip drooping. Then she turned back to Amelia. ''Do you think they'd have an outfit in my size?''

Amelia smiled through tears. Love overflowed for the dear little woman who'd not only accepted what she'd done without blinking an eye, but was now ready to try her own hand at it.

''Aunt Rosie, you'd be precious. But don't you think that the hours are a bit too late for you? After all, it was very late by the time I got home and into bed and you know how you hate to miss your beauty sleep.''

Anticipation faded from Rosemary's bright blue gaze. Her backbone slumped and she sighed. ''You're probably right. I must have my sleep. It's vital to a healthy digestion, you know.''

''Yes, ma'am,'' Amelia agreed.

''Well!'' Wilhemina said. ''I can't say that I'm perfectly pleased with your choice of job, but I can't see anything wrong with it. After all, if that library board hadn't been so penurious, you would never have been forced to such measures. And I have a sneaking suspicion that our neighbor across the street has been telling tales. I should give her a piece of my mind!''

''Just let it be, Aunt Witty. It's all my fault for sneaking out. Surely the rumors will die down soon. At least I hope they do. I don't think I can stand many more days like today.''

And then to Amelia's dismay, she started crying all over again. Wilhemina ushered her up the stairs, reassuring her all the way that they were not upset with her.

Rosemary stared as they disappeared into Amelia's room. She was so furious with that Effie Dettenberg she could hardly think. For two cents she'd…

And then a thought occurred. If Amelia was having trouble with the men in this town, then another man should be the one to fix it. Poppa always said that men should fix what they broke.

She pursed her lips, fluffed her hair, and headed for the kitchen. A ring of keys hung by the bank calendar. With determination in every motion, she slipped them from the peg and headed out the back door.

A twinge of nervousness sparked as she slid the key into the old blue Chrysler's ignition. It had been a while since she'd driven a car. But, she reminded herself, it's like anything else. Once you've learned a task, you never truly forget it.

The motor fired up with one small pop. She stretched, trying to reach the clutch and realized that Amelia had the seat scooted as far back as it would go. She sighed. It would have to do. She was on a mission and didn't have time to be adjusting seats.

Jerking and coughing, the car's engine did its best with the instructions it was receiving. With no small amount of luck, she managed to reverse from the driveway. Unfortunately for the Chrysler's gears, she then shifted into high instead of low. When she accelerated, the car took off down the street with tires squalling. She made the turn at the corner with a grin on her face and the wind in her hair.

Maurice had started across the street in search of a mouse when the huge machine came barreling toward him. Hair on end, claws digging into the pavement, he made

the curb and safety just in time. Even though he was no
longer in danger, even though the horrible noise was long
gone, he kept running and didn't stop until he'd reached
the small dark space beneath the porch. Eyes wide with
fright, whiskers twitching, he hunkered down beside the
brick footing and growled his best growl. Just when he
needed her, his mistress was nowhere in sight.

Tyler parked the tractor inside the shed and climbed
down a dusty and weary man. Cultivating peanuts was a
thankless but necessary job. He stretched and then reached
for a grease rag and a wrench. It was his habit at the end
of each day to service the tractor so that it would be ready
for the next day's work. He'd just begun when he heard
the sound.

At first he thought he'd imagined it because there was
a brisk breeze blowing. A bucket hanging against the opposite wall banged intermittently as the wind whipped
through the doorway. He shrugged and turned to check the
oil when he heard it again. This time he dropped the grease
rag and walked outside. Standing quietly, he tilted his head
into the wind and listened.

Someone was obviously driving at a high rate of speed.
He heard the boards on the bridge across Sumter Creek
rattle as the vehicle evidently flew over it. He walked a
few steps farther into the sunshine and then staggered from
shock as he saw a familiar old blue car top the rise above
his farm.

It was Amelia, and she was driving so fast! A little spurt
of fear settled in his belly. Something must be wrong! And
then he remembered that she had her new car. Why, he
wondered, was she back in the old one?

The car skidded sideways, sending dust flying into the
wind as it made the sharp turn into his driveway. Frowning, he started toward the house when he noticed that the
top of the driver's head was barely visible above the dash-

board of the car. That's when he recognized the driver and began to run.

"Hello, Tyler Dean. It's a fine day isn't it?"

"Miss Rosemary." It was all he could say as he yanked the door open and told himself not to drag her from the car. "What the hell—excuse my language—are you doing? Has something happened to Amelia? Why didn't you call? I would have come into town."

Rosemary brightened perceptibly. She'd known that he'd be the one to help. She hadn't even said a word and already he was inquiring after Amelia's welfare.

"I'm so glad that you asked, Tyler Dean. I just didn't know what else to do, you know. After Amelia started crying and all, why, I…"

He froze. Amelia? Crying? A sharp pain pierced his heart as the thought sank in. He couldn't bear the idea of Amelia in pain, whether it be physical or mental. He grasped the elderly woman by the shoulders, turned her toward him, barely managing to ask without shouting.

"Why was Amelia crying, Miss Rosemary?"

Her mouth drooped and her eyes glittered angrily. "It was all that Effie Dettenberg's fault, I just know it. She's been telling tales on Amelia, you know. Amelia took an extra job to earn money for her car and…"

He sighed. So she'd finally confessed to her aunts. He wished to hell she'd do the same to him. However, he had to admit that their situation was a bit different.

"How do you know someone told?"

Rosemary repeated what Amelia had said.

Tyler grew silent. His face paled and then flushed with anger.

"You mean…she's been experiencing this everywhere?"

The curls on Rosemary's head bobbed vehemently as her own indignation continued to rise. "Oh, yes! She said the man who pumps gas asked her if she had a special rate for Saturday nights. The boy at the grocery store pinched her on the—'' she blushed and lowered her eyelids ''—you know, and people whisper constantly. She's just devastated.''

His lips tightened and it was all he could do to swallow his rage. He slipped his hand beneath Rosemary Beauchamp's tiny arm and ushered her toward the house.

''Come with me, Miss Rosemary. I've got to change clothes before I take you home.'' When she would have argued about that idea, he stalled it with a small white lie. ''I don't think you should drive the car until I check it out. I heard a funny noise as you were turning into the drive.''

He didn't have it in him to tell her that what he'd heard was the bumper of her car taking down his mailbox. He'd fix that later tonight after he got her home.

Rosemary was all for doing her own thing, but fixing cars wasn't within the realm of her understanding. ''Oh, well then, I'd be pleased. And I'm so glad we had this talk. I'm sure you'll know just what to do.''

''Yes ma'am,'' Tyler said shortly. ''I know just what to do.''

In just under thirty minutes he had her back home. He watched with relief as she doddered safely inside the house, then he rolled his eyes and grinned. Now he knew where Amelia had gotten her sense of adventure and independent spirit. At the same time, the thought of Amelia also reminded him what else was at hand. He drove down to Main Street with a fire in his eyes that was very reminiscent of his younger days.

Rosemary burst into the kitchen as a puff of wind lifted her skirt. ''Did you hear?''

''Shut the door, Rosemary. It's windy,'' Wilhemina complained. ''And did I hear what? Do hurry and sit down. You took an awfully long walk. We've been waiting breakfast for you.''

Amelia looked up from her orange juice and stared.

There was a gleam in Rosemary's eyes she couldn't ever remember seeing.

Rosemary sighed and took her seat. "If you don't want to hear about the fight, then I guess I'll…"

"What fight?" Amelia and Wilhemina echoed simultaneously.

Rosemary smiled and leaned back in her chair. She had the floor and fully intended to do the story justice.

"Well, yesterday it seems that Tyler Savage drove up to the gas station, crawled out of his pickup truck and punched Henry Butcher in the nose. They say…" she paused for effect "…that he whispered something in Henry's ear and then left him bleeding all over the concrete. They also say that Henry just stood there and took it, like he knew he had it coming, you know."

Wilhemina frowned. She didn't approve of fighting.

Amelia's heart thumped. Something told her there was more to this story than Rosemary was letting on. "What else did they say, Aunt Rosie?"

Rosemary beamed. "Then, *they* said he drove up to the grocery store, walked into the back and cornered that young boy who always carries out groceries—you know— I think it's Jewel and T-Bone Armitage's oldest boy." She took a deep breath. "Anyway, they said that he threatened the boy within an inch of his life and left him throwing up from nothing more than pure panic. He didn't lay a finger on him. Just talked, you understand."

Amelia could almost guess the rest of the story. Something told her that Tyler had gotten wind of what had been happening to her. She also knew that the aunts had a terrible row last night just after Rosemary had come home. She'd been in her room, but she'd heard enough to know that Rosemary had actually taken the car and driven it out of town. Still sick at heart about her own misfortunes, she'd fallen asleep before she learned how Rosemary had gotten home. This morning, she'd looked outside and seen that her Chrysler was still missing. After what Rosemary just said, Amelia suspected that she must have caught a ride with a savage named Tyler.

Wilhemina frowned. "I must say, I don't hold with all that violence. Still…" She looked at Amelia strangely. "I wonder what set him off like that?"

Amelia blushed.

Rosemary looked down at her plate. "Are we having pancakes?" She'd delivered her news, she was ready to eat.

Wilhemina sighed. Knowing her sister, that was all the sense that would come out of her for the day. "Yes, Sister. We're having pancakes. And you didn't wash up after you came in, did you?"

"Why, no! I don't believe I did. I'll be right back. Save the first stack for Amelia. She won't want to be late for work." She left the room in a flurry.

Amelia ducked her head and stared at her plate. She could hardly face the idea of going back to the library and dealing with people who talked behind her back.

Wilhemina saw her niece's nervousness. She pursed her lips and leaned forward. "You don't give them an inch, do you hear me, Amelia Ann! Let them talk. We know the truth."

Amelia blinked and tried not to cry. She'd sworn to herself that she'd cried enough on the subject. "Yes, ma'am, I hear you. And I won't cry. Not anymore."

"Good!" Wilhemina said. "Now, come help me fix the pancakes or you'll be late. We don't want anyone to think you're hiding, do we?"

Amelia stopped and then stared, as if seeing her aunt in a different light. "No, ma'am. I wouldn't hide. Beauchamp women don't hide, do they?"

The old woman paused, pancake turner in hand, and then looked back at her niece. "I don't know about that, my dear. If we hadn't hidden from the truth that times change and life goes on, you wouldn't have been driven to deceit, would you?"

There was nothing to else to say. Wilhemina went about the business of pancakes while Amelia considered what they'd just shared. For one brief moment, she almost smiled. Something told her that this was only the beginning. She could hardly absorb the meaning, but it would seem that Tyler had fought for her. It was something straight out of one of her romance books, and it had actually happened right here in Tulip!

Tyler's reputation had hit an all-time high. It was all over town that he'd actually fought for Amelia Beauchamp, that he'd taken the gossip floating around Tulip about her as an actual insult and decided to rectify the situation. Needless to say, the gossip ceased almost instantly.

Effie Dettenberg was just the least bit nervous that Tyler would actually appear on her doorstep and do something equally dastardly. And, her conscience *was* troubling her about what she'd caused, but righteous indignation kept her from admitting it. The way she looked at it, if you ate the spice, you paid the price. It was only fitting.

Amelia's reputation had also taken on a new twist. In a small way, she'd actually become Tulip's latest femme fatale. It was unbelievable what gossip could do to a woman's life.

Tyler took a last look at himself in the rearview mirror of his pickup truck before he got out. He was as ready as he'd ever be to face his future, and that's what he'd come to consider the three Beauchamp women. He'd already admitted to himself that he didn't want to face a life without Amelia, and she came with two ready-made chaperones. That was fine with him. He'd take Amelia Ann any way he could get her. With a determined jut to his chin, he pulled up in front of the old two-story home and parked, then grabbed the bouquet of flowers he'd just purchased at the local flower shop. When he reached the front door, he knocked twice and waited.

Wilhemina answered. For one long moment they stared into each other's eyes. Judging. Measuring. Tyler was the first to speak.

"Miss Wilhemina, I know I should have called, but I'm the type of man who prefers to face situations head-on. I've come to ask your permission to court your niece, and these are for you."

It was reflex that made her take the offered bouquet. But it was pure pleasure that made her sink her nose into the huge cutting of yellow gladiolus. How had he known she liked the spiky blooms?

"Well now," she muttered. "I suppose you'd better come in."

Tyler's belly settled just enough to answer. "Yes, ma'am. I suppose I should."

Amelia hadn't been home from the library more than half an hour and was upstairs changing her clothes, unaware of the momentous meeting taking place downstairs. The day on the job had gone better than she'd hoped, but she was still a bit lost as to where she stood with Tyler. Granted he'd come to her aid when she'd asked for help about buying a car. And, it *was* a fact that he'd actually had a fight, almost two, over her reputation. But she had yet to know what his intentions were.

Too tired to worry about it any longer, she shrugged out of her dress and reached for a pair of white slacks and a matching long-sleeved blouse. They were old, but soft and comfortable. She was digging in the bottom of her closet for a pair of low-heeled, sling-back sandals when her aunt's voice drifted upstairs.

"Ahmeelya!"

"Coming."

The last thing she'd expected to see was Tyler at the foot of the stairs, watching her descent like a cat waiting for a mouse to emerge from a hole. Then she saw the look on his face and nearly missed a step. She was out of her hole. What he intended to do with her was another matter altogether. By the time her foot touched the bottom step, she was a nervous wreck.

"Amelia."

His voice was soft and coaxing and it pulled her the rest of the way toward him. She wanted to fly into his arms just as she had on more than one occasion at The Old South, but this was Tulip, and she was Amelia, and so she simply looked at him and smiled.

"Tyler's staying for supper," Wilhemina said shortly.

Her mouth dropped as she turned and stared at Wilhemina in shock. If her aunt had announced she was running for mayor she wouldn't have been more surprised.

He could hardly take his eyes off the tall, elegant young woman dressed in white. He desperately wanted to take her in his arms and kiss that worried expression on her mouth. "Only if Amelia has no objections," Tyler reminded her.

Wilhemina snorted. "That's unlikely," she muttered. "Amelia, you help me set the table. Rosemary will entertain our guest until the meal is ready to be served."

Amelia had a moment of panic at the thought of Aunt Rosie alone with this man. What in the world might she say? She was capable of almost anything. And then she remembered. If what she suspected was true, Aunt Rosie and Tyler had already established a relationship of sorts. They'd probably do just fine.

"Yes, ma'am." She shrugged and grinned at Tyler. There was no use arguing with Aunt Witty. "Where is Aunt Rosie, anyway?"

"I don't know, but I expect she'll be along soon. I heard her go out a few minutes ago. She's probably gone for one of her walks."

Then Wilhemina turned to Tyler, suddenly a little confused as to what to do with him. "Well, young man, I suppose you know how to turn on the television. I'll call you when supper is ready.''

''Yes, ma'am,'' Tyler said. He was just as vulnerable as Amelia. He didn't know where he stood with this woman, but he'd do anything it took to get in her good graces.

He watched them leave the room and then shoved his hands in his pockets and grinned. This was a hell of a note. Tyler ''Give 'em Hell'' Savage was parked in the front parlor of a one hundred and fifty-year-old house trying to get on the good side of a woman in her eighties just so he could make time with the niece. He'd never spent so much time worrying about approval in his entire life.

Dutifully, he turned on the television and took a seat. This was going to be a night to remember, he could just feel it.

Across the street, Effie Dettenberg was also receiving an unexpected guest as she went to answer the knock on her door.

''Why, Rosemary, do come in! I can't remember the last time you came to visit.''

''Thank you, Effie, but I believe I'll just stand out here. This isn't a social call.''

Effie blanched and then blustered. She wasn't going to be put out by a diddly-headed old woman fussing at her. Effie completely ignored the fact that a mere three years separated them in age. She'd done nothing wrong. Absolutely nothing at all.

''Then state your business,'' Effie said. ''I've got to get Maurice's supper. He doesn't like to be kept waiting.''

Rosemary fluffed herself up to her full height of five feet three inches, patted her hair and smoothed down the skirt of her pale blue organza.

''I understand you've been meddling,'' she said sharply. It was so unlike Rosemary to be sharp about anything that Effie was momentarily dumbstruck.

"I don't know what you're talking about," Effie said. She stared over Rosemary's shoulder, half expecting to see the older sister come charging across the street.

"That figures," Rosemary said. "You rarely know what *you're* talking about, either, so let me make myself clear." She took a step forward and pointed a dry, shaky finger in Effie's face. "If it were me, and I'd been the one who'd snuck out of my father's house to run away with a riverboat gambler years ago, I wouldn't have the nerve to talk about anyone else's business. But it wasn't me who did that, was it, Effie?"

Effie drooped against the door frame and considered the possibility of just slamming the door in her face, but that wouldn't help matters. From the look on Rosemary's face, not much would. She gulped and tried to talk. Nothing but a hiss came out as Rosemary continued.

"I *heard* that your father went looking and found the both of you in a cathouse in Natchez. I always figured that was just gossip. I hate gossip, don't you?"

Effie groaned.

Rosemary straightened her shoulders, glanced down at the watch pinned to her bosom and grinned brightly. "Well now, it's nearly suppertime. I do believe we're having pot roast tonight, and it's my favorite. I wouldn't want to be late." She started down the steps when she stopped and turned. "I'm so glad we had this talk, aren't you?"

Effie nodded and watched the tiny woman dodder across the street, then sucked in a breath. It escaped slowly through her teeth in a near-silent whistle. She'd just been sideswiped by Hurricane Rosemary and considered herself lucky to still be standing.

By the time she realized that she should be suffering some sort of indignation, she slammed the door a bit too late to impress anyone and stomped toward the kitchen.

"Darned old biddy. Didn't think there was anyone left in Tulip old enough to remember."

Effie's one bid for freedom had ended in supreme defeat

and embarrassment. She'd spent her adult life trying to live down the event by bringing everyone else's reputation down with her. Obviously, she was going to have to find a new outlet for her energy.

Eight

Rosemary patted at her hairdo and succeeded in mussing more than fixing. "I just can't remember the last time we were escorted into Sunday services. This is so exciting."

Tyler grinned as Amelia calmly put Aunt Rosie's hairdo back in order. "Yes, ma'am," he agreed. "It's real nice for me, too. I don't normally get to sit with three pretty women."

The phrase "pretty women" pleased Wilhemina. But no one would have been able to tell from the prudish expression on her face. Her mouth puckered disapprovingly as she watched Tyler slip his hand beneath Amelia's arm. And then a strange and unfamiliar emotion tugged at her heart as Amelia's face lit from within at Tyler's touch. For a moment she wondered what her life would have been like if she'd done things differently. She sighed.

"Yes, well, it's been a while since a man occupied our family pew. I suppose it's time."

Rosemary twittered and giggled as Tyler slid his other

hand beneath her arm and helped her past a crack on the step.

Wilhemina frowned at her sister's girlish flirting. It was close to a disgrace. "Rosemary! Do come along."

The aunts moved ahead, leaving Amelia and Tyler a few steps behind. Glad that she had a moment alone, Amelia turned to say something to him and forgot what it was when she walked into a kiss.

Tyler couldn't help himself. It was the glimpses he kept getting of Amber that reminded him of what lay beneath Amelia's virtuous exterior. Her mouth was warm and open, and he took outrageous advantage of the opportunity to slip inside.

Amelia was just starting to enjoy it when she remembered they were standing on the church steps in full view of anyone who happened to be arriving. With a reluctant blush, she pulled back, and then glanced around, sighing with relief as she realized there was no one in sight.

Tyler traced the fullness of her lower lip with the tip of his finger as his eyes traced the outline of her body. He'd never realized how enticing a woman could be by revealing less, not more. It was a puzzling realization to know that Amelia was even more intriguing than Amber.

"I'm not going to apologize for that," he said, and then grasped her by the arm and quickly ushered her inside the church, only a few steps behind the aunts.

That the congregation took notice of his seating arrangements was putting it mildly. The whispers were rampant until Tyler made what looked to be a nonchalant turn toward the congregation. The shut-up or put-up look he gave them was clear. Tyler Savage was openly courting Amelia Ann Beauchamp and there wasn't a man alive in Tulip who had enough grit in his craw to argue the issue.

For Amelia, the worst of it was over. For Tyler it was just beginning. He had to figure out a way to convince Amelia that he really loved *her*, and knew it wouldn't be easy. After all, she'd also heard him tell Amber how much she meant to him. If he wasn't careful, she'd think him a philanderer. She didn't know he'd caught onto her "other life."

It would all be so simple if she'd just confess, but he could see her point. She'd have to look him square in the face and admit that she already knew how hard his body got when he held her. That she moaned exactly twice every time he kissed the spot below her chin where her pulse throbbed. And that her breasts always peaked beneath that red satin just from his look.

He'd experienced a side of Amelia that she had yet to admit existed. It was strange to have almost made love to one woman and barely gotten past kissing another—and they were still one and the same.

When the preacher called for the first song, Effie hit the chords at the organ with unusual force. Rosemary looked up from her hymnal. Obviously Effie had gotten the message. It was good that she'd chosen to put her fervor into religion for a change. Rosemary was of the opinion that a little change never hurt anyone. With a satisfied smirk, she straightened her skirt and patted her hair in place. It was a wonderful Sunday after all.

The last crumb of Wilhemina's coffee cake disappeared into Tyler's mouth. He leaned back and groaned with a satisfied smile on his face.

"Miss Wilhemina, you're a fine cook. I haven't eaten as much or as well since my folks moved to Florida."

She almost blushed. "Thank you, Tyler."

The thought of having a man to a meal at their house had been horrifying to her, but now that it had happened, she realized it hadn't been nearly as bad as she'd expected. After all, he'd asked so politely to come courting, it was only good manners to respond in kind.

Amelia smiled and then caught a look from Tyler that froze the smile on her face. If she knew her man—and she'd spent the last fifteen years of her life absorbing as much knowledge of him as she could—food was the last thing on his mind.

His eyes caressed her body with a look that sent a wave of heat spiraling to her face, but she gave back look for look, allowing herself a rare exploration of the man who'd stolen her heart.

While she watched, his lashes wavered and then slowly lowered. She watched his nostrils flare as his eyelids closed. It was subtle, but the shift of his fingers into a fist was obvious as his napkin crumpled in the palm of his hand. The buttons on his shirtfront tightened and pulled against the fabric; the only hint he'd given that the breath he'd just taken was long and deep. But when he opened his eyes, the fire inside made her flinch.

With shaking hands, she tried to return her water glass to its proper place and clinked it against her plate, instead. The aunts looked askance, half-expecting the remaining contents to go spilling across the linen tablecloth. Amelia blushed, caught it as it teetered and righted it with a whisper of apology.

Rosemary tried not to giggle. She'd seen the looks passing between them and knew what was going on. My, but it was going to be nice having a man around the house.

Innocence dripped from her voice. "My word, Amelia, it's such a nice afternoon, you should take Tyler for a drive in your new car. Get a little fresh air into your lungs. You know how you've been having those headaches."

Wilhemina frowned. She didn't think it was a good idea. But she hesitated too long and there was no easy way to insert her objections as Tyler quickly picked up on the suggestion.

"You have headaches?" His concern was genuine.

Amelia shrugged. "Some."

"She reads too much," Wilhemina accused.

Rosemary rolled her eyes. "For pity's sake, Willy. It's her job. What would you have her do, guess at the contents of the books in the library? When someone comes in asking her a question she can't answer, would you have her lie? I'm surprised at you."

Wilhemina glared. Her concern for the unchaperoned trip was forgotten as her anger at her sister increased. Unknowingly, she'd fallen right into Rosemary's trap. Her gasp of outrage was loud and long.

"I'd never have her lie!"

Amelia caught the gleam in Aunt Rosie's eyes. Why, the little schemer! She's done this on purpose just to distract Aunt Witty from causing a scene about Tyler!

Tyler knew something was afoot. He could tell by the stunned expression on Amelia's face. He didn't know what was up, but he had no intentions of losing the advantage of Rosemary's invitation.

"Amelia, I'd be pleased if you'd let me do the driving. I'd like to show you my farm. The crops are up and the weather's been holding. This promises to be a good harvest."

"That would be fine," she said, and tried not to bolt from her chair.

Wilhemina's eyes grew round. She started to splutter when Rosemary sighed and leaned forward, accidentally on purpose upsetting a jar of conserve. The spoon that flew out onto the white linen was sticky with the sugary cherries.

"Oh Willy, just look what I've done! Help me get these dishes off before it leaves a stain."

Wilhemina jumped to her feet and began removing the plates while Rosemary turned and winked at Tyler. It was so charming and so unexpected, he almost laughed. He just realized what Amelia had spotted instantly. They had a cohort in their budding romance.

"Run along you two," Rosemary urged, as her sister disappeared into the kitchen with a stack of china. "When she comes back, I'll tell her you gave her your regards. What she doesn't know won't hurt her."

Amelia threw her arms around Aunt Rosie and nuzzled

the rose petal softness of the weathered little cheek. "I love you," she whispered.

Rosemary's blue eyes twinkled as she whispered back. "You're telling that to the wrong person."

Amelia was dumbstruck. Love Tyler? Could that be true? In a daze, she allowed Tyler to lead her away.

Tyler opened the door, helped her into the seat of his truck, and then moved her skirt away from being caught in the door. Inadvertently, his hands ran the length of her thigh as he scooted the fullness to safety. Even below the folds of yellow fabric he could feel the firm, slender legs she dutifully kept hidden. He swallowed harshly, remembering what they'd looked like beneath the black net hose Amber always wore, and looked up. She was staring back, with lips parted, breathing soft and enticingly urgent. Unable to resist what she offered, he leaned forward, and in the front yard in front of God *and* Effie Dettenberg, he kissed her.

Amelia moaned as that sexy mouth invaded her space. Firm lips enticed...cajoled...promised. She gripped the seat with her hands and shuddered as he slowly withdrew.

"Are you ready, darlin'?"

She blinked. Ready? Was she ever! "Oh, uh, yes!" A wave of pink swept across her cheeks. "We'd better go before Aunt Witty realizes we're still...that we..."

Tyler laughed. "Darlin', if your aunt knew what was on my mind, she'd never let you out of the front yard."

Amelia was so stunned by his honesty that they drove all the way out of town and through several miles of countryside before she realized that they'd turned into the driveway of his home and had parked.

"We're here," Tyler said.

"So we are," she said breathlessly, and looked everywhere and at everything except Tyler.

For one long moment they sat in shared silence inside the pickup truck while Tyler watched the confusion in her expression coming and going. That plus her stiffened posture told him all he needed to know.

She was nervous.

But hell, she had nothing on him. Every muscle in his body was jumping like frog legs in a frying pan. He wanted to drag her out of that pickup, coax her into his arms and into his bed and never let her out of the house again. All he could do was offer her a hand down from his pickup.

Amelia fidgeted with her skirt and hair, wishing she had a mirror, then in quiet panic, smoothed down the collar of her dress and started to straighten her belt when Tyler's hand stayed her intent.

"Amelia…"

With a sigh, she looked up.

"Darlin', please don't be afraid of me. I would never do anything to harm you. I'd fight snakes to keep you happy."

Amelia relaxed and then smiled, remembering that he'd already fought for her. He just didn't know that she knew.

"I know that. But this is so strange. We've lived in the same town forever, yet until now, you've never seemed to notice me." She blushed, but continued. "I knew you. I just didn't think you knew I existed."

Tyler pulled her across the seat until they were so close she could see her own reflection in his eyes.

"Try not to judge me by my past stupidity. Unfortunately, it often takes a man a good while longer to grow up than it does a woman. Fortunately for us men, you women often have the patience and wisdom to wait." He traced the edge of her chin with his forefinger. "I can't thank you enough for waiting."

Amelia shivered in his arms. "You're welcome."

The scent of his cologne was heady, as was the sight of that mouth only inches away from her face. She could remember what it'd felt like earlier when he'd kissed her in her front yard. Dear Lord, but she wanted more from him than kisses. The man was making her crazy.

Tyler took her by the hand. "Come on, Amelia, if we don't get out of here, we're going to get into trouble."

Amelia followed his command. That kind of trouble would come later...but it *would* come. Of that she was certain.

And so the afternoon passed as they walked, and looked, and listened to each other. Tyler's nonstop monologue about his farm, his family and his love for the land had been an eye-opener for Amelia. The man was more than just a pretty face and a sexy body. Oh, she'd known he was industrious. And it was obvious that he was successful. But today had opened another facet of Tyler to her. When it came to things that belonged to him, he was downright possessive. It was an intriguing thought.

Amelia wondered how important a woman would be to a man with so many responsibilities. She also wondered how a man like Tyler would feel saddled with three more responsibilities. It was a point she had to consider. In her case, two elderly women would always have to be a consideration. She would never be able to abandon them and their welfare for the love of a man, not even if it was Tyler Savage. He'd have to love and accept them, too, or their relationship would never work.

Amelia sighed, letting her head rest against the porch swing as she waited for Tyler to come out of the house. He'd gone in a few moments earlier to get them something cold to drink, leaving her rocking in the shade of his back porch.

Tyler's hound lifted his head to sniff the air, then dropped it back onto his front paws and closed his eyes. Amelia smiled at the red dog's lassitude. It was an enticing picture. Before she knew it, her shoes had slipped off her feet. The cool afternoon breeze tickled her toes just enough to make her curl her feet beneath her in the seat. The dog yawned then rolled over on his back. Amelia grinned at the way his head lolled one way and his body another. She stretched her arms above her head, slid her glasses off her nose, and slipped down in the seat of the swing.

Tyler stood at the kitchen door, a frosty glass of lemonade in each hand as he stared through the screen, watching Amelia sleeping. Moisture condensed on the outside of the glasses and ran between his fingers. He shuddered and swallowed once as he watched her breasts rise and fall with each breath she took.

Abandoning the lemonade to the kitchen table, he walked quietly outside onto the porch, lifted her glasses from her limp fingers and laid them on the porch rail then slipped into the swing beside her. And then her head was in his lap and his fingers were in her hair.

She sighed once, her eyelids fluttering against her cheeks as Tyler's heart twisted with an emotion that nearly staggered him. With quiet skill, he ran his fingers through her hair for the pins holding it in place, and each time he found one, released it from its mooring. One by one, Amelia's curls began to fall out of place.

When he had finished, he stared down at her, a handful of her hairpins clutched tightly in his fist. She moved unexpectedly and he dropped the pins just in time to catch her before she fell out of the swing and onto the porch.

She looked up at him in confusion and made him want her beneath him, so hot and desperate that she didn't know whether to breathe or scream. Instead, he pulled her across his lap. Her hair tumbled across his arm as he cradled her against his chest. When he buried his nose in the curls sun-heated warmth, he inhaled the faint scent of Amelia's shampoo.

''Don't fight me,'' he whispered, and then sighed with relief as he felt the tension receding from her body.

His fingers traced the softness of her arms, up and down, from elbow and to the curve of her shoulder. She moved once, tentatively sliding an arm around his neck and when she did, his hand slipped across her breasts.

Her swiftly indrawn breath did nothing but expand the swell beneath his fingers, pushing her against him until he thought he would die from the want. She shifted nervously in his lap, uncertain whether to move closer or farther away.

He was too damned close to the breaking point to ignore her hips digging against the ache in his lap. "My God, Amelia, don't move."

She froze. His warning had come in the same instant she'd realized where she was sitting. She might be inexperienced, but she wasn't dead. And there was no denying the fact that what she was sitting on was not soft. In fact, it felt downright uncomfortable.

Tyler relaxed as her wiggles ceased.

Right about then, Amelia realized her appearance had taken a drastic change from when she'd sat down in the swing. Her hair was heavy against her neck and back, and the slightly fuzzy edge to Tyler's face told her she was no longer wearing her glasses.

In a panic, she bounded from the swing, spied her glasses on the porch rail and swiftly shoved them in place. Grabbing at the flyaway locks, she gave him an accusing look. "My hair! What happened to my hair?"

Tyler tried not to grin. "A couple of pins fell out, and I helped the others."

Amelia was afraid to look at him. *What if he recognizes me? What if this day wasn't the beginning of our relationship, but the end?*

Tyler sighed. He knew what had prompted her panic. It was guilt. *Tell me, girl. Tell me now.* But she didn't speak, and time passed, and finally he leaned over, picked up her hairpins and quietly handed them to her.

"Here, honey. There's a bathroom down the hall, first door on your left. Help yourself to my brush and comb."

She grabbed the pins and made a dash for the door. It slammed abruptly behind her as Tyler watched her flight.

"Oh, Amelia, all you have to do is tell me."

He buried his face in his hands and tried not to think about the pain in his lap. It was nothing to the one in his heart.

The drive home was uneventful. Amelia was back in place, and, so was Tyler. He'd retreated, leaving her space in which to breathe. She sat closer to him, but purposefully refrained from talking about anything personal.

When they pulled into the driveway, Tyler jumped out and quickly ran around to the passenger side of the truck. The aunts were sitting on the veranda in matching wicker chairs with a pitcher of lemonade on a small table between them.

Tyler helped her down from the truck without speaking.

Amelia knew that her behavior had been irrational, but at this point, explaining herself seemed impossible. Instead, she brushed her hand across his arm and smiled. "I loved going with you today. I loved the tour of your farm and…"

"I personally loved your nap the best."

She blushed and then smiled. "I was getting to that," she said, surprising him by her candidness.

"Yoo-hoo!"

They turned toward the house.

"We're being paged," Tyler said, as Rosemary waved to them from her chair. "I'd better make my apologies and get back home. There's evening chores to be done."

He walked her to the porch, smiled at the twinkle in Rosemary's eyes and ignored the frosty look of censure in Wilhemina's.

"You were gone all afternoon," she accused.

"Yes, ma'am. It's a very big farm."

She was slightly mollified by his remark. After all, there was nothing to be said about the truth.

"Look!" Rosemary muttered. "There's that Effie Dettenberg staring at us from her window."

Tyler turned to look. He could see the curtains pulled back and a dark, shadowy figure standing to one side. His eyes narrowed. He knew good and well that she was the initial cause of the gossip flying around Tulip about Amelia, and it made him mad as hell. He shoved his hands in his pockets and glared, wishing she wasn't a woman.

And then his eyes narrowed as he considered the thought that just popped into his mind. Before Amelia saw it coming, Tyler turned and grasped her by the shoulders. There in the front yard, in front of the aunts and Effie Dettenberg, he calmly kissed Amelia goodbye.

She was so staggered by his daring she did nothing but smile as he turned her loose.

"Goodbye Amelia," he said. "Miss Wilhemina, thank you again for the wonderful meal. Miss Rosemary, it's been a pleasure."

Rosemary grinned. She stared back across the street and waved at Effie's house, knowing full well that Effie could see everything going on.

Wilhemina was shocked. She nodded her acceptance of his praise, but she was embarrassed by his behavior. The man had a nerve, yet a small satisfaction had come at his daring. At least he'd announced his intentions like a gentleman, and he *had* kissed Amelia here in plain view. It wasn't as if he was trying to hide his feelings for her. She sniffed. She didn't particularly like men, but if one had to be hanging around Amelia, she supposed that Tyler Savage was as good as the next. Satisfied that she'd come to a sensible conclusion, she sent a withering glance across the street and felt a swift surge of delight as the curtains suddenly fell back in place.

Amelia's face was glowing and her heartbeat was completely out of rhythm. Somewhere between Tyler's farm and her home she'd finished falling in love. There was no power on earth that would keep her from this man. Not now! Not when he'd just shoved his opinion of Effie Dettenberg in Effie's face. Not when he'd had the nerve to kiss her in front of her aunts, knowing full well the censure he might receive.

Tyler had just given her a message. What she did with it now was up to her. He'd made his intentions as plain as possible.

Amelia watched him walk away and then knew she couldn't let him go...not without a word.

"Tyler!"

He stopped, surprised by the fact that she was even willing to speak to him after the public way he'd bid her goodbye. He knew that a lot of her aunts' stiff-necked propriety was deeply imbedded in her, regardless of the yearning she had to stretch her horizons. He turned and waited.

"I had a wonderful time today."

His smile was slow in coming, but when it did, it curled Amelia's toes inside her shoes.

"It was my pleasure, Amelia. Absolutely, my pleasure."

Oh no, Amelia thought as he drove away, I had my share of the pleasure, too, Tyler. Remembering the way his hands had moved across her body and the pressure of his mouth against hers, she shivered. Maybe more than my share.

As Amelia drove into the grocery store parking lot, she saw Raelene Stringer struggling with two bulky sacks of groceries and losing ground with the hold she had on a sack of potatoes dangling from a two-finger grip. And Raelene's old car was nowhere in sight. She frowned. Something told her that it had finally given up the ghost.

She jumped from her car, grabbing at a sack just before it fell on top of the potatoes Raelene had already dropped.

"Looks like you've more than got your hands full."

Raelene grinned. "I'm surprised you've got the guts to be talking to me. I've been hearing things about your reputation that put mine to shame."

Amelia pretended to glare. "If you'll shut up and get in, I'll take you home. What happened to your car?"

Raelene sighed with relief as Amelia helped her load

her packages inside the shiny red car. As she slid into the passenger seat, she wiped a hand across her forehead.

"Oooh, honey, I do appreciate the ride. That car is a mess. Although I'm on foot for the day, it's in the garage and should be ready by this evening."

"No more than I appreciated the rides you gave me," Amelia said. "And the friendship...and the loyalty...and..."

Suddenly embarrassed that Amelia was still willing to claim a friendship even after all that had happened from their previous association, Raelene muttered. "Well, hush your mouth. I didn't do anything."

"No, not much," Amelia said. "You just kept your mouth shut and stayed a friend. It's more than these self-righteous, upstanding members of Tulip's finest managed to do."

Her bitterness was obvious. Raelene glanced sideways as Amelia turned down the side street leading to her duplex. "Has it been rough?"

Amelia rolled her eyes. "Did Sherman march through Georgia?"

Raelene grinned. "At least you haven't lost your sense of humor, girl, and, from what I hear, you haven't lost that Tyler, either." She giggled as Amelia turned into her drive and parked. "How did he take the news?"

Amelia gripped the steering wheel as a look of guilt spread across her face. "I haven't told him." Raelene's shriek of disbelief echoed as she quickly continued. "But I'm going to. The first time I can work it into the conversation, I'm going to tell him...I swear."

Raelene stared at her friend. It was her personal opinion that Amelia Beauchamp was as naive as they came. How could she possibly believe that Tyler didn't know she was the same woman? He'd obviously held them both. If Raelene knew her men—and she did—he'd surely kissed Amber and Amelia.

She snorted beneath her breath and tried not to laugh.

Tyler knew. He had to. Amelia was the one who was still fooling herself. And then she shrugged. She'd survived by not butting into other people's business and now was no time to change. She opened the door and got out.

"I can't thank you enough for the ride," she said, as Amelia helped her carry her groceries to the front stoop.

Amelia paused. "Just returning a favor to a friend."

Raelene stopped in midstep, then stared. It was true! For the first time in her life she had a friend, and it was a woman who didn't judge her, but simply accepted.

Tears filmed her heavily painted eyelashes and she blinked them away as she dug into her purse for her house key.

"Well, now, I suppose that you're right. Thanks for the ride, honey. You're a peach."

"Anytime," Amelia said quietly. "Anytime."

Raelene knew as she watched the little red car turn the corner that Amelia had meant it. It was a good feeling to know that in a pinch there was someone to whom she could turn. She also knew that she'd never use the opportunity, but it was satisfying to know it, and Amelia, were there.

Nine

Rain splattered against the windows in bulletlike projectiles, driven through the night by the intensity of the storm. Amelia awoke with a start and sat up in bed, surprised by the suddenness with which it had arrived. A tree limb knocked against the corner of the upstairs roof and she winced, knowing that tomorrow there'd probably be shingles lying in the yard. An unwelcome, but unavoidable, expense.

Thunder rumbled, rattling the panes of glass as the storm passed swiftly overhead. A sharp tinkling sound came from downstairs.

"Oh no, not a window!"

She reached for her bedside lamp and then frowned. The power was off! As she jumped from her bed, she scooted her feet into slippers and headed downstairs to investigate, pausing only long enough to get a flashlight from the hall table.

The thin beam of light from the flashlight illuminated

little more than a five-inch circle of space—not much to
go on in the dark. Halfway down she heard a heavy thump
followed by a low moan of pain.

"Oh no! Aunt Witty! Aunt Rosie!"

She pivoted in place and ran back up the stairs, her
floor-length nightgown billowing out behind her. When
she burst into Aunt Rosie's room and saw her sitting in
the middle of her bed with a frightened, befuddled expression on her face, she breathed a quick sigh of relief.

"Aunt Rosie…are you all right?"

Her chin trembled. "I think Willy fell," she said, and
started to crawl from her bed.

"Don't move," Amelia ordered. "The lights are out and
I don't want you to fall, too. Stay where you are. Please!
I'll be right back."

She ran across the hall, using the flashlight to guide her
way. The beam of light was weak, but it was enough to
see Wilhemina stretched out upon the floor, her ankle tangled in the sheet dangling from the side of the bed while
a thin trickle of blood ran down her forehead.

Amelia knelt at the old woman's side, searching the pa-
per-thin skin on her wrist for a pulse. It was there!
Thin…but steady. "Oh, Aunt Witty…please talk to me."

"Amelia?"

The voice was weak, and shaky, unlike the Wilhemina
she knew and loved.

"I'm here, Aunt Witty. Don't move. I'm going to get
you some help."

And then Rosemary called out. "Is she hurt? Tell her
I'm coming."

"No, don't," Amelia shouted. "Wait for me." She ran
back across the hall, fearing that Rosemary would try to
navigate in the dark and suffer the same consequences, and
caught her just as she started out the doorway.

"Come with me," she urged, using her flashlight to
shine the way. "You've got to stay with Aunt Witty while
I call for help. She's fallen and hurt her head."

"Oh my!" Rosemary gasped, and then started to cry.

"Aunt Rosie!" Amelia's voice was so loud and sharp, so unlike any tone she'd ever used, that Rosemary forgot she'd been about to cry.

"You can't go to pieces on me now. We need you."

Rosemary sniffed several times in succession as she adjusted herself to the news, meekly allowing Amelia to lead her across the hall. Once inside the room, Amelia got a pillow from the bed, seated her aunt Rosie upon it and then handed her a washcloth.

"Here, press this gently against the cut. I'm going to call for an ambulance."

Rosemary took the cloth and did as she was told while Amelia disappeared down the hall. For the first time in their lives Wilhemina was not in charge, but then she heard Amelia's footsteps on the stairs and breathed a sigh of relief. Amelia would take care of everything. She was a very capable woman.

Wilhemina stirred beneath her hands.

"Rosemary…is that you?"

Rosemary clutched the thin hand that crept into her own as she continued to press the cloth to the cut on her sister's forehead.

"Yes, Willy, it's me. Now lie still, darling. Amelia's gone to get you some help. You're going to be just fine."

Amelia raced to the phone, using instinct rather than good sense to find her way through the darkened rooms. She set the flashlight on the table, shining it so that she could see to dial, and picked up the receiver. The line was dead!

No electricity…no phones! How was she going to summon help?

"Oh no, oh no," she muttered, and fought back panic. There was nothing for her to do but go for help.

She dashed back upstairs, stumbling twice in the darkness as she missed her step. By the time she got back to the bedroom, Rosemary had pulled herself together.

"Willy's talking to me, dear. Her head doesn't seem to be bleeding any longer, but she's hurt her ankle. Is the ambulance on its way?"

She took a deep breath, trying not to let her panic show. "The phones are out, too. I'm going to my room and dress, and then drive to the police station downtown. They can contact help for us."

Wilhemina reached urgently toward her niece. "No, Amelia! It's storming. You might have a wreck."

"I'll be fine. Just promise me you'll lie still."

"She'll do as I say," Rosemary said quickly. "We won't budge, dear. I trust you to do the right thing."

"I love you both," Amelia said. With a quick brush of her lips across their fragile cheeks, she was gone.

In a way, her life as Amber had trained her to dress and undress in the dark. It was a help now as she tore off her nightgown and then struggled into her jogging outfit. Grabbing her sneakers, she dropped to the floor to put them on, her hands shaking as she struggled with the laces. Then with flashlight in hand, she took the stairs three at a time, her long legs covering the distance as she made a dash for the front door.

But when she got outside, a streak of lightning across the sky showed her that she wouldn't be driving anywhere. The driveway was blocked by a fallen tree. Without hesitation, she leaped from the porch into the storm and began to run.

Thunder rumbled. Tyler rolled over and sat straight up in bed, staring around his darkened room and wondering why he'd awakened in such a panic. His heart was pounding as if he'd been running, and although the air was almost chilly, sweat was pouring from his back and chest. Before he thought, he'd grabbed the phone and was dialing Amelia's number. And then he slammed the phone down in disgust. No dial tone. The lines must be down.

He reached for the lamp and cursed softly as the switch

clicked without illumination. He rolled over to the edge of
the bed and then sat, ignoring the darkness and trying to
mask the overwhelming fear that kept running through his
mind.

"Something's wrong, I just know it."

He got to his feet and walked to the window. Rain pep-
pered against the panes as he looked out into the storm.
The peanuts needed a good rain. Now he wouldn't have
to irrigate for a while. If he was lucky, maybe not at all
before digging started. But the good news of much needed
moisture did nothing to quell his fears. He kept telling
himself that it was nothing for the phones to go out when
it stormed. He couldn't figure out why he was in such a
panic. Granted he couldn't communicate with anyone, but
who would he call at this time of night, anyway? He raked
shaky hands through his hair, trying to talk himself out of
the panic. What had he been thinking about when he'd
started to dial Amelia? If the aunts had gotten a phone call
in the middle of the night, it would have scared them to
death.

"Well, hell," he muttered, pulling on a pair of jeans as
he headed for the kitchen. There was no way he'd be able
to go back to sleep with this feeling of doom hanging over
him. Maybe if he got something to drink it would take the
feeling away.

Coffee was out of the question. With no power, he had
to settle for a cold bottle of soda pop from the refrigerator.
He unscrewed the lid and took a drink, then walked outside
and stood beneath the shelter of the porch to watch the
rain.

The fierce winds had calmed. There was nothing left of
the onslaught but a constant downpour. The earth smelled
fresh; newly washed, dust-free and replenished as the thunder rumbled far to the south. The storm was gone, but the
feeling he'd awakened with was not.

He leaned against the porch post as he drained the last

of the cola and knew he was about to do a foolish thing. But when a man was in love, fool was his middle name.

He headed indoors. Even in the dark, the empty bottle he tossed in the trash hit with unerring aim as he headed for his room to dress. He had to see a woman about some peace of mind.

"Is she going to be all right?" Rosemary asked again.

Amelia hugged her aunt's tiny shoulders and tried not to cry. They'd been waiting for what seemed like hours outside the emergency room where Aunt Witty had been taken.

"I'm sure she is, Aunt Rosie. It just takes time to get X-rays made and then have them read. You know how slow things like that are."

Rosemary knew, but until she saw her sister's face and heard her order someone about, she wasn't going to feel good about this at all. Not at all.

"Have you called Tyler?" she asked.

Amelia shook her head. "The phones must still be out. I kept getting a busy signal and I know he's not on the phone at this time of night."

"He won't know where we are," Rosemary worried.

Amelia tried to smile. "It won't matter. We'll be home before he ever knows what happened. Besides, we're not his responsibility, Aunt Rosie."

Rosemary stared at her niece as if she'd taken leave of her senses. "But of course we are, dear. He loves you, you know. He'll want to know what's happening to us. That's what people do who care for each other."

Amelia smiled through tears. Aunt Rosie's outlook on life was so naive. Amelia had already had a suitor who'd abandoned her for greener pastures when he'd been faced with the fact that his girlfriend had responsibilities he didn't want to assume. Her and Tyler's relationship was new. They'd had no time to test their feelings for each other. The word "love" had not even been mentioned, although she'd sensed it was there. And Amelia still had to face the possibility that he might not like the facts, once they were pointed out to him.

And then something made Amelia look up. It was Tyler! And he was running down the hall toward her with a look on his face that sent her flying into his arms.

"How did you know?" she cried.

He shivered as he wrapped her in his arms. "Beats the hell out of me, darlin'. All I know is, I woke up in a cold sweat and started running."

Amelia pulled away in shock. "You what?"

"Never mind." He cradled her face in his hands. She was here in his arms and she was safe!

"See, dear, I told you he'd care."

Tyler turned. In spite of Rosemary's determination to remain positive, he could see the strain the night had put on her.

"Come here," he said, and held out his hand. She sidled into his embrace as if she'd been doing it for years. For a long moment, the two women stood, sheltering within the strength of Tyler's arms.

"Does anyone know how Wilhemina's doing?"

Amelia swallowed a shaky sob. "We don't know. They've been working on her for such a long time and no one's come to tell us anything."

He frowned and then feathered a quick kiss across her brow. "I'll be right back," he said. And headed toward the nurse's station wearing a look Amelia wouldn't have wanted to face.

Rosemary looked up and tried to smile. "Tyler will fix things, won't he, dear?"

Amelia sighed. "I hope so, Aunt Rosie. I certainly hope so." But she knew there were only so many things a man could fix. She couldn't bear to think of the consequences if Aunt Witty didn't get better. She was a third of her world.

A short time later, Tyler was back and the news he had was positive.

"She has a mild concussion and a twisted ankle, and nothing's broken."

"Thank the Lord," Amelia whispered, pointing to Rosemary who'd fallen asleep on the waiting room sofa.

He hated to tell Amelia that more was needed of her this night. He could see she was nearly at the end of her rope. Her eyes were too bright. Her lips too firm. She was obviously close to a breaking point herself, but it had to be done.

"They want to keep her overnight but she's giving them fits. I think they need your help to settle her down."

She glanced back at Rosemary, who was still sleeping like a baby. "Would you keep an eye on Aunt Rosie? It won't take me long. I promise I'll…"

Tyler grasped her by the shoulders. "Darlin'! Stop it! Of course I'll stay with her. What did you think I'd do? Walk off and leave her to wake up alone?"

Amelia stared at a point just over his shoulder and tried not to cry. She couldn't admit that she'd feared this episode would only assure Tyler he'd bitten off more of a courtship than he wanted to swallow.

"Don't you know how much you mean to me?" he asked.

She shrugged.

Tyler shook her gently. "When this is all over, Amelia Ann, I think we've got some talking to do. But for now, go calm down your Aunt Witty. I'll wait."

It was the single best thing he could ever have said. He'd wait! Overjoyed, Amelia threw her arms around his neck and kissed him soundly on the mouth before she hurried away.

Tyler sank down onto the sofa at Rosemary's feet and tried not to grin. This whole mess was close to hopeless, but his love for Amelia was not.

It was almost four in the morning when they pulled into

the driveway. Amelia was wide-eyed and pale with shock, and Rosemary was asleep in the seat. He leaned forward, pressing a soft, sweet kiss at the corner of Amelia's mouth.

"I can't park any closer to the house, but I can furnish delivery service."

While Amelia watched, he lifted the tiny old woman into his arms, cradling her gently against his chest. "You get the door, sweetheart. I'll carry her upstairs. There's a flashlight in the glove box. Watch your step."

Rosemary barely stirred. The night had been too wild and traumatic for a lady in her eighties.

As they entered the house, Amelia breathed a sigh of relief. At least the power was on! She led the way as Tyler carried Aunt Rosie upstairs.

Rosemary awoke as they entered her room, a bit confused as to how she'd gotten here, but glad that they were back. Yet uppermost in her mind was her elder sister's welfare.

"Is Willy all right?" she asked, as Amelia put her to bed.

"Yes, darling, now let me help you with your robe. I think you should sleep in tomorrow. I'm not going to work. If we don't deserve a day off for this, we'll never deserve one."

Tyler watched from the doorway as Amelia tucked the old woman beneath the covers. But when she turned out the lights and closed the door behind her, she fell into his arms.

He held her close, running his arms up and down the damp sweatshirt she was wearing as she shivered beneath his touch. "You're so cold, sweetheart, and your hair is still damp. You need a warm bath and a bed, yourself."

She leaned forward and wrapped her arms around his waist, too exhausted to think about consequences.

"I will after a bit," she said. "There's a broken window downstairs. I need to…"

"Get in the tub," he ordered gruffly. "I'll sweep up the

damned glass and find something to cover the opening until we can get it fixed tomorrow. It's too dark to worry about anything else tonight. Okay?''

We *can get it fixed?* It was the most wonderful sound in the world. Amelia had never expected to hear those words coming from a man's lips. Suddenly she had someone to count on besides herself.

Her lower lip trembled. It was enough to send Tyler's blood pressure rocketing.

''Sweetheart,'' he groaned, and tilted her chin. They touched. Mouth to lips…heart to heart…man to woman. And it was not enough. His arms tightened.

Amelia knew this man wanted everything from her that she was willing to give and tonight was not the time.

Tyler was the first to pull away and he thought that it might kill him. He ached to make her his. He wanted this beautiful woman beneath him in his bed. He wanted to go to sleep with her cradled in his arms and wake beside her every day for the rest of his life. He wanted her in his life forever and whatever it took, he was willing to wait.

''Get in the tub, woman. If I didn't have to sweep up your mess, I'd join you.''

Too tired to blush, she staggered to do his bidding. With a heavy heart, she stripped off her clothes and stepped into the shower. The fact that one of her aunts was in a hospital and the other was asleep in a bed just down the hall made no difference tonight. There could be no lovemaking between them as long as Amelia's lie remained. She had to find a way to tell him that the woman he'd been attracted to as Amber was also Amelia. He'd haunted the workplace of one woman and then come courting the other when the first had turned him down. How was he going to feel about her deceit? She turned her face into the shower spray and ignored the tears flowing with the water. If she didn't tell the truth soon, fate might have the last laugh on them both.

It would be just her luck if Tyler decided he didn't want
either woman, and Amelia and Amber lost the only man
they'd ever loved.

"Did you get it all cleaned up?"

Tyler turned. The woman standing on the stairs was like
something out of a dream. Her hair billowed around her
face and down her back like a rich chestnut cloud. Those
beautiful blue-green eyes stared at him, wide and anxious
with questions he couldn't—didn't dare—answer. The
long nightgown she was wearing drifted just above the
tops of her bare feet and although she was covered from
neck to ankle in the softest and finest of white fabric, she
was sexier than Amber had ever been in that little bit of
shiny red spandex.

He dropped the broom and dustpan and walked to meet
her. She stood a step above him on the stairs and when he
came within reach, she wrapped her arms around him, hugging cheek to cheek.

"I'll never be able to thank you for tonight and all
you've done."

He could feel her breasts, soft and pliant as they pressed
against him. His hands spanned her waist, gathering the
gown and its voluminous folds around her as he enfolded
her within his arms and pulled her from the stairs.

He groaned. "I can think of several ways, and all of
them are impossible tonight."

Amelia sighed. She knew he was right, but it hadn't
been what she'd wanted to hear.

"Come with me, sweetheart. You need to get in bed,
too. I'll tuck you in and lock up on my way out, okay?"

She nodded. Whatever Tyler said was good enough for
her.

To her surprise, he lifted her in his arms, and although
she was nearly twice her little aunt's height, he carried her
back up the stairs as if she weighed nothing at all.

The door to her room was open. He paused on the

threshold, staring at the empty bed. "Oh, hell, this wasn't such a good idea."

Amelia had succumbed to exhaustion and barely heard what he said, but when he lay her down on her bed, she stared back up at him, watching…waiting.

Tyler's eyes narrowed thoughtfully. He knew if he asked, she would not tell him no. But he couldn't and wouldn't ask.

With no small amount of determination, he pulled the sheets out from under her feet and covered her up.

As she rolled over, she exhaled slowly, her eyelids drifting downward as comfort and exhaustion drew her deeper into their spell.

"Amelia…"

The tone in his voice drew her back from the edge of sleep. The word "what" was on the edge of her tongue when he finished what he'd started to say.

"I love you. Get some sleep."

She watched him walk away and knew that what he'd asked would now be impossible. After saying that he expected her to sleep? Men were such fools.

"Tyler."

Tyler turned. "Yes?"

"After telling me something like that, you don't honestly expect me to sleep, do you?"

His heart skipped a beat.

"What do you mean?

"How quiet can you be and still make love to me?"

"Quiet?"

The look on Tyler Savage's face was somewhere between stunned and starving. Amelia stifled a grin.

"Yes, you know…as in do not shout or grunt at an inopportune moment?"

Tyler swallowed nervously. He wasn't certain but he was damn sure willing to give it a try. He glanced at the closed door across the hall, picturing the shock on the little old lady's face should she know what they were considering.

"Absolutely not," he whispered.

Amelia hesitated, then slowly turned back the covers and patted the pillow beside her head.

"Are you sure this is okay?" he added.

Amelia sighed. "Right now, the only thing I'm sure of is that I'll regret it if you leave."

A small smile tilted the right corner of his mouth as he closed and then locked her door.

"Well, now…it's against my code of honor to cause a woman any sort of regret, so move over, darlin' and make room for me."

Tyler toed off his boots and then reached for his belt buckle. When he turned around, Amelia's gown was lying at the foot of the bed. He knew there was something he should say, but before he could form another complete thought, she'd put a finger to her lips to remind him to stay quiet, then turned off the light.

His heartbeat thundered against his ears, but he didn't know how to quiet his heart. When he slid into bed beside her and wrapped his arms around her, the softness of her skin and the fragility of her body next to his made him weak with longing. He nuzzled the spot beneath the lobe of her ear and then whispered against her cheek.

"Close your eyes, darlin' and just let yourself feel the love."

And so she did.

From the first tender touch of his lips against her skin, she was lost. The romance in the books that she read was nothing compared to the weight of his body pressing her against the soap-fresh scent of the sheets, or the firm and knowing stroke of his fingers as they sought out her most private secrets. Other than the occasional catch of a breath or the soft exhale of a sigh, the room was absent of sound. Outside, the storm was passing, but the storm within these walls had only begun.

Tyler waited to take her until he was half out of his mind and when he finally allowed himself the luxury of sinking into her warmth, he had to stifle a deep groan. Then he started to move, rocking back and forth against the sweet woman's body as she took him straight to heaven.

Sometime just before dawn, Amelia felt Tyler slipping out of her bed and then heard the soft rustle of clothing as he began to dress. When she felt his mouth against her forehead, she smiled. The door opened, then closed. Satisfied that for now, all was right with her world, she hugged the sheet to her chin and before she knew it, it was nearly ten o'clock in the morning and Rosemary was bustling into her room to drag her from bed.

Ten

____

"**W**hat do you mean…men are at the door?" Amelia asked, as she pulled her nightgown over her head and staggered from her bed and into the bathroom with Aunt Rosie at her heels. Thankfully, Aunt Rosie failed to notice Amelia had been naked in bed.

"Oh, it's okay. Tyler's in the kitchen. He'll take care of everything. I tried to fix him some breakfast but he said he'd already eaten." Pleased with her news, she smiled as Amelia turned to stare at her.

Water dripped down Amelia's face onto her gown. "You cooked?"

Rosemary nodded, then frowned. "It wasn't the same as Willy's, though. I never did have the knack. I either forget to salt or sugar something, or add too much of each." She shrugged. "I lose count, you know."

Amelia grabbed for a towel and began drying her face, thankful that Aunt Rosie hadn't set the house on fire. The last time she'd tried to cook, a potholder had gone up in smoke. Her first instinct was to panic, but she hugged her little aunt instead.

"Now, Aunt Rosie, you have other qualities that are special. I don't know anyone with your knack for growing flowers."

Rosemary beamed. "You're right! I do them well, don't I!" She fluffed her hair, straightened the Peter Pan collar on her green silk chiffon, and headed for the door.

Besides the fact that Rosemary was wearing one of her better dresses, there was a distinct priss to her walk. "You're certainly dressed up this morning."

Rosemary paused at the door. "Yes, dear, we have callers, you know."

It reminded Amelia of the fact that there were strange men meddling about their premises and decided that haste would not be amiss. There was no time for her fussing. Bothering with a dress and fixing her hair took back seat to the fact that Tyler was in her kitchen. She grabbed for her glasses as she dug through her closet in search of a pair of slacks and a blouse. Minutes later, Amelia came flying into the kitchen, wild-eyed and breathless, then came to an abrupt halt as the man standing at the kitchen sink turned and smiled.

"Tyler, there's a man at the door with a chainsaw,"

With a smile, he reached for her, wrapped his arms around her, and gave her a swift, but promising kiss.

"Good morning to you, too, darlin', and the man with the saw is a neighbor of mine. I told him he could have the wood if he'd move the tree from your driveway. This way it won't cost you anything, and David will have some firewood. Was that okay?"

Amelia accepted his kiss as well as his explanation, but began to panic. All of this upheaval was in progress and she'd been asleep in bed, letting him bear the brunt of the burden. She shrugged out of his grasp and waved her arms around the room. "It was more than okay, and I appreciate all you're doing…but I don't want you to feel obligated or pressured in any way to deal with all of this mess.''

The look on her face made him want to shake her. Even after last night, she was putting that wall back up between them that he'd spent weeks trying to break down. He frowned.

''Damn it, Amelia Ann, the only thing that's bothering me is the fact that you keep pushing away my offers of assistance. I'm not going to ask for my payment in flesh.'' And then he smiled and added. ''Again.''

It took a moment for his inference to sink in and then when it did, a soft pink flush crept up her face.

Tyler sighed. He'd be damned glad when she got past whatever nemesis she had that kept her from telling him the truth about her double life. Then he took her by the hand and began coaxing her into an easier frame of mind.

''Never mind, honey. Why don't you come outside with me, okay? I want you to see what the men are doing. David is removing the fallen tree, Elmer from the hardware store is replacing your broken window and the insurance adjuster is on the roof assessing the damage to your shingles.''

Amelia followed. There was nothing left to do. It seemed as if Tyler had thought of everything. And then she remembered.

''Oh, wait! I want to call the hospital and check on Aunt Witty.''

''I'll be outside. Come out when you're ready.''

Amelia dialed and then waited nervously to be connected. She couldn't believe that after she and Tyler had made love, that she'd simply fallen asleep as if she had no duties at all to attend. And then her toes curled against the ends of her shoes as she thought of making love to Tyler. He'd said he loved her but she hadn't said it back. Couldn't until she told him the truth. Oh Lord, how did I make such a mess? She chewed her lower lip as she counted the rings and leaned against the wall, listening to the activity outside the house. She didn't want to face the turmoil and kept struggling with tears, wondering why she was so tired and depressed. All she wanted to do was crawl back in her bed, with Tyler, and never come up for air.

The fact that she'd run halfway across town at night in the middle of a storm and then had to deal with both aging women should have been enough reason for her. But Amelia'd had too many years of self-sacrifice built into her system to accept the fact that she was only human.

Finally someone answered the phone, and the firm, no-nonsense voice that pricked her ear made her weak with relief.

And from the sound of it, Wilhemina was in no mood for conversation.

"Aunt Witty? Is that you?"

"Of course!" she snapped. "Who else would be answering the phone in my room, and why aren't you here?"

Amelia sighed and then smiled. Her Aunt Witty was back! "Because I just woke up," she said, and then grinned even wider as her aunt began to fuss. "Aunt Witty...Aunt Witty, please listen to me for a minute. I'll be there as soon as possible, okay? I can't come get you until I can move my car, can I? There's a tree down across the driveway, the insurance adjuster is here and someone is fixing a window. As soon as they all leave, I'll be along."

Wilhemina slumped back against her pillows. She recognized the wisdom of her niece's words. She just hated being in an unfamiliar place having people she'd never seen in her life poke about her body. It wasn't seemly.

"Well, all right then," she muttered and moved on to other concerns. "How is Rosemary? You know she never can make a decision without my help."

Amelia hated to confess, but she'd learned long ago never to conceal things from Wilhemina Beauchamp. Invariably she always found out.

"She cooked."

Wilhemina gasped. "Lord have mercy! Don't leave her there by herself when you come to get me. Bring her along or we won't have a house to come home to."

"Yes, ma'am." Outside, she heard a man's loud laughter and knew she'd left Aunt Rosie alone with the opposite sex too long. "I'd better go, Aunt Witty. Aunt Rosie's already outside with the repairmen. I'll see you soon."

"Not soon enough," Wilhemina mumbled.

"I know, Aunt Witty," Amelia said. "I love you. Take care."

The phone disconnected in Wilhemina's ear. But it didn't stop her from answering her niece's last words. "I love you, too, dear," she said. "I just didn't know how much until now."

Wilhemina hung up the phone and lay back on her pillow, remembering only bits and pieces of last night's episode, but remembering enough to know that were it not for Amelia, there would have been no ambulance, and no one to take care of Rosemary or see to the house while she was gone. She didn't know what they'd do without her. As she settled in the bed, she thought of Tyler Savage and frowned. She didn't want him in their lives. If he came and took Amelia away, what would happen to them?

It was a selfish thought, and Wilhemina would have been appalled to admit she had a selfish bone in her body. She tithed regularly at the church and always volunteered for community affairs. She'd given up her life to care for Rosemary. And then later, Amelia. She wouldn't admit that she'd had no life except for them. She'd shut off everything and everyone who could have possibly made a difference. And she'd done it because she was afraid.

Effie stood at the edge of the yard clutching Maurice to her chest as she watched the goings-on at the house across the street. She'd give her eyeteeth, if they were still in her head, to be over in the middle of the action. But she'd pretty much worn out her welcome by flapping her mouth and she knew it.

She watched as a man pulled a chainsaw from the back of his pickup truck and walked over to the fallen tree blocking the drive. She saw him staring the length of the tree as if assessing the damage, but she wasn't prepared when he pulled the cord. As the saw started, the insistent whine sent Maurice scratching and scrambling out of Effie's arms and running for cover beneath the porch.

She frowned and muttered as her beloved pet made his getaway. When she looked up her disgust turned to fear. Rosemary was coming across the street!

Effie's greeting was less than friendly. It was hard to be kind to someone who knew where all the skeletons in your closets hid out. "Rosemary."

Rosemary nodded.

"Willy will be home today. She has suffered a mild concussion as well as a sprained ankle. We will be needing some daily help while Amelia is at work and I wondered if you'd be interested? I remembered you used to stay with Mrs. Abercrombie after the Mister passed."

Effie gawked. "You want *me* to stay in the house with you?"

"Only during the day," Rosemary said. "We couldn't pay much, but we'd…"

"I'd be pleased," Effie said. "And I don't need pay. After all, what are neighbors for? And it's not like Wilhemina's going to be bedridden or anything."

Rosemary beamed. "Fine then. Amelia will be going back to work tomorrow. We'll see you around eight?"

Effie tried to contain her pleasure. After all, it wouldn't be seemly to be receiving joy from someone else's misfortune. But the fact remained, she was excited to be spending a few days in someone else's company other than Maurice's. She'd always wanted Wilhemina's recipe for coffee cake. Maybe she'd share. Then she remembered the look of disdain Wilhemina had given her last Sunday after church services and decided not to push her luck.

Across the street, Tyler saw Amelia coming out of the house and waved at her to get her attention.

"Amelia! Over here, darlin'."

She blushed, embarrassed that he'd called her darling in front of at least three other men, yet pleased that he'd done it.

He slid an arm across her shoulder and aimed her attention to the adjuster who was just coming down a ladder from his excursion across the rooftop.

"How's it look?" Amelia asked.

The adjuster brushed off his hands and squinted back up at the roof. "Not bad. Most of the damage is on this side of the house. The worst is here at the corner where the tree caught it as it fell." He glanced at the shiny red car only a few feet away from outstretched branches. "Good thing your car wasn't parked any closer to the house. It would have nailed it for sure."

Tyler smiled at Amelia and hugged her gently. "She's more than earned this car. It would have been a shame to have it ruined after all she's been through."

Amelia jerked; a slight and surprised reaction to what Tyler had just said about what she'd "gone through" to get it. He smiled at her, absently ruffling her hair before helping the adjuster slide the ladder back in his pickup truck, but she was still in a quandary. What had Tyler meant by that? If he knew something...surely he'd have mentioned it before now?

Nervously she turned to look at him, and then forgot what she'd been thinking. As he lifted the ladder out of the adjuster's way, her breathing caught. Watching his muscles flexing and his thighs harden as he braced his legs to balance the load reminded her she'd been held in those arms. She also knew what his mouth felt like when it moved upon her lips and neck with gentle abandon. She shivered, remembering what it felt like when he was on top of her—and inside of her—and then nearly fell into Aunt Rosie's flower bed at her own impertinence.

Rosemary gasped. "Amelia! Watch out for the impatiens. They're so delicate. What could you possibly be thinking, dear? That flower bed's been in the same place for years. Please be more careful." She bent down and swiftly patted a chunk of soil back in place as Amelia staggered out of the planted plot.

You don't want to know what I was thinking. It's definitely X-rated, just like that man.

"Sorry, Aunt Rosie."

She looked up just in time to see Tyler coming toward her from across the yard. For some reason, she panicked. Maybe it was a combination of too many men on the premises and not enough sleep, but her reaction to the grin on his face was unexpected.

"Now then," Tyler began. "As soon as the…"

"We can handle it," Amelia said. "There's no need for you to bother yourself any longer with our business."

The shock on his face was apparent. She groaned. At that moment, she would have liked to yank her tongue from her mouth and toss it to Maurice who was skulking just outside the fence across the street, but it was too late. Tyler had already taken offense and she didn't blame him. She was pretty disgusted with herself, too.

"Bother?" The tone of his voice deepened as his eyes narrowed to slits of fury. "You think I've been *bothered* by helping someone I care about?"

"I didn't exactly mean…"

"Never mind, Amelia," he said shortly. "You may be right. Hell, I know you are!"

He grabbed her by the shoulders and shook her slightly to get her attention. But it *was* unnecessary. He already had it.

"You hit the nail right on the head, Amelia Ann. You've been *bothering* me from the first time I noticed there was a woman beneath that plain brown wrapper you're hiding in. I'm bothered all day. And darlin' let me tell you, the nights are hell! But…'' He dropped his hold and glared ''…you should get down on your knees and thank the Lord I finally got your message. If someone *bothers* you again—it damn well won't be me.''

He stomped across the yard, slammed himself and his pickup into gear and drove away.

Amelia would have followed him. She would have called out that she was sorry and begged his forgiveness, but she couldn't. There was a huge knot hanging at the back of her throat that made breathing difficult, never mind speaking. And the tears in her eyes blinded her to any and everything except the fact that the she'd just insulted and rebuffed a man she loved.

''Oh my!'' Rosemary said as she noticed him driving away. ''I didn't even get to tell him goodbye.''

Amelia looked back at the house, past the fallen tree and the men's curious stares. ''Neither did I, Aunt Rosie. Neither did I.''

And then she burst into tears.

The women settled into a routine that went surprisingly well. Wilhemina had been incensed by her sister's presumption that they needed help, and even worse, that she'd asked that gossip Effie Dettenberg to do it. But from the first day, the odd association of females had clicked. Amelia went to work each morning just as Effie came across the street toward their house. They'd wave in passing. For Effie it sufficed. For Amelia it was all she could manage.

Wilhemina then proceeded to run the household from an easy chair while Effie and Rosemary kept the rest of the place in passable order. Effie cooked and cleaned and Rosemary stayed out of the way.

Nearly everything was back to normal. Everything, that is, except Amelia's life. It had come to an abrupt halt when Tyler left, and she hadn't seen him since. It had been eight of the longest days in her life. She'd spent the days in

distress and the nights in torment. When she wasn't think-
ing of him, she was dreaming of the man. Her body ached.
Her heart hurt. She knew what she needed and it was
Tyler.

Amelia shoved a book into its proper place on the library shelf and sighed with relief. Quitting time! She
headed for the washroom to freshen up, but she wasn't
going home, at least, not at first. She wasn't spending another sleepless night remembering the look of pain she'd
left in Tyler's eyes.

She leaned close to the mirror, blinking rapidly as she
tried to adjust to the contacts she was wearing now instead
of glasses. They had been a necessity, not a daring move
on her part.

Last night she'd put her owl-eyed frames on the sideboard right after their evening meal. When she'd come
back from doing the dishes they were nowhere to be found.
When she'd asked, Rosemary had looked vaguely guilty,
but Amelia figured they'd eventually turn up. Aunt Rosie
was always losing something, whether it belonged to her
or not.

Amelia took down her hair and gave it a thorough brushing before gathering it at the nape of her neck with a ribbon that matched the turquoise slacks and blouse she was
wearing. She'd already called home and asked Effie if
she'd stay long enough to get the aunts into bed without
going into details. It wouldn't do to tell the only woman
in town who had hinged jaws that she was going out to a
man's house to beg for forgiveness.

So she locked the library, got into her little red car and
headed out of Tulip. She had to see a man about her life.
It was on hold until he smiled at her again.

Tyler slammed the back door as he entered the house.
Another long day at work had passed only to come home

to an equally long night alone. He glared at the contents
of his refrigerator and then shut the door with a sigh. He
didn't want to eat. He wanted Amelia.

It had been eight of the longest days of his life since
he'd left her standing on the front lawn of her home. He'd
come to the conclusion that if anything ever worked between them, it would have to be at Amelia's choice. And
so he'd waited and waited, and she didn't call, and each
day his confidence waned until he physically ached for the
sound of her voice.

He shrugged, unbuttoned his shirt, and headed for his
bedroom and a warm, welcome shower. If he was going
to be miserable…he'd do it clean.

Amelia parked her car and sat for a moment, hoping
that Tyler might come out. But the door didn't open. The
big red hound beside the porch didn't even bark. She felt
unwanted and unwelcome and disgusted with herself for
being so hesitant about something this important.

"Okay, this is it," she muttered. "Either he'll forgive
me or he won't. He gave up on Amber out of disgust. He
may give up on me, too, out of frustration."

Her chin quivered and her lower lip trembled while tears
pooled, liquid shimmer on a blue-green surface. Her knees
went weak as she got out of her car and started toward the
house. When her footsteps echoed loudly on the wooden
porch, it startled the hound into one weak carol that ended
in a snuff of disinterest.

Amelia knocked, and then started to pray.

Water from his shower was still clinging to his body
when the first knock sounded.

"Hell!" Tyler said. "It never fails."

He grabbed at a pair of clean jeans and pulled them on
his still damp body, fumbling with the buttons as he
yanked a shirt from his closet and headed down the hall.
His bare feet made a pat-pat sound as he hurried to the

door, but when he yanked it open, he forgot what he'd been about to say.

A wall of pain hung between them as Tyler stared at the woman on his doorstep.

Amelia held her breath, waiting for him to make the first move, but the look on his face frightened her even more than she already was. Pooling tears finally overflowed.

The tears were more than he could stand. He dropped his shirt and held out his arms. "Come here," he groaned, and pulled her into his house and into his arms, kicking the door shut behind him as he held her close.

"I'm sorry. I didn't mean to..."

His mouth stopped the rest of her apology and nearly her heart. She was soft in his arms and pliant to his demands, and she had on too many clothes for his peace of mind. His hands shook as he lowered her feet to the floor. It had been heaven holding her. Turning her loose was going to be hell.

His hands cupped her face. His fingers lovingly traced the gentle contours of her cheeks and chin before traveling down the fragile curve of her neck. "I'm awful glad to see you, darlin', but I need to know why you're here."

Amelia nodded. That was fair. She rested her forehead against his chest, trying to find words to say what was in her heart. But his skin was hot and his body was hard and she was finding it difficult to think. She wanted inside this man's world in the very worst way. Finally, she just slipped her arms around his waist and leaned back in his arms, the better to see his face.

"I came to say I'm sorry."

He relaxed and pulled her lower body tightly against him.

"What else?" he asked and moved once against her.

Amelia moaned as her eyelids dropped. This was why she'd come, but was she ready for this?

"What else, Amelia?" he repeated. His voice deepened

as his hands moved slowly up and down her body, coaxing the answer from her slightly parted lips.

"I need to tell you that I..."

He moved again. Only harder. A gentle thrust between friends and lovers.

"Oh!" Her eyes flew open as she looked into promises she needed him to keep.

"Tell me what?" he persisted, and moved again. Only this time he moved away then smiled gently as she followed his retreat.

"Tell you that you're driving me crazy. That I don't know what I'm doing from one minute to the next. That I can't sleep. I can't eat. I..."

They were as close as clothing would allow. "I get the message. Do you get mine?"

She started to shake, but walking away from this man and what he wanted from her was impossible. Her pulse raced as she traced the band of muscles across his chest, lingering longer on the wild rhythm of his heart. Her eyelids fluttered as she accepted the powerful swell of his lower body pushing at her boundaries, then with a heartfelt sigh, she took his hands and placed them on her breasts.

When she filled his palms, he groaned. Moments later, she was in his arms as he carried her down the hall, never taking his gaze from her face. With a reverent kiss, he lay her down upon his bed and then stood back. She lowered her eyes, suddenly shy of the man who'd stolen her heart, although she knew it was time to show him how much she cared.

Tyler sat down beside her and tilted her chin. "Don't, Amelia. Don't turn your face away from me—not ever again. No more secrets between us for as long as we live, okay?"

She jerked as if he'd slapped her. Secrets! There was still one awful one hanging around her neck that needed to be told.

"Tyler, there's something I should..."

But he slipped off her blouse and she forgot what she'd been about to say, and when she was lying upon his bed staring at the magnificence of his body, she lost what was left of her mind. There was nothing left in their world but sight, and touch, and gentle whispers that promised heaven.

The small foil packet he took from a drawer was his last rational act, because when her arms lifted and encircled his neck, he slid between her legs and tried very hard not to die from the joy.

Breathing came in the form of one short gasp of pleasure after another, rocketing through a world of rhythmic motion. There was nothing but a white-hot need that kept on burning as they loved and made love.

Amelia was lost in a world of emotions and sensations. His hands on her body, his weight an anchor to the splintering fire that kept teasing her sanity. His mouth coerced as his body demanded. She took everything he was willing to give and then more. And then the pace changed—intensified to the point of blinding passion as she cried out his name.

Tyler heard her but was too far gone to speak. He gave her the only answer of which he was capable. With a final thrust, he sent heat spiraling throughout her body and waves of pleasure that ebbed and flowed until she was limp beneath him.

Her soft shudders gave him joy. He buried his face in the valley between her breasts to hide a smile. She might be shy on foot, but in bed she was more woman than any man had a right to expect.

With a low, weary moan, she buried her fingers in his damp black hair. "Tyler...Tyler."

"Is that all you can say, darlin'?" he said, then smiled when she blushed.

Amelia looked into his eyes, treasuring the love she saw there, knowing it shone for her. There was plenty she should say to this man, but now was not the time. What just happened was out of a dream. He had stolen her heart long ago, and now he had her. For the first time in her life, she knew what it meant to love, body and soul.

"Oh, Tyler, it's all I *can* say, at least for now. But later, we have to talk."

He knew what was troubling her, and to tell the truth, was a little apprehensive about her confession himself. When she finally admitted that she'd been living a double life and had actually dated him as both her alter ego and her true self, he was going to be in a bit of a fix. How was he going to explain that he'd been on to her almost from the start and not make her angry?

He groaned beneath his breath and held her close. Hell! Being in love was not easy.

"Tyler?" Amelia's voice was hesitant, nearly a whisper against his cheek.

"What, darlin'?"

"Could we do this one more time…before I go?"

He burst out laughing as he rolled her into his arms and rolled them both across the bed, tangling their arms and legs in the process.

"It would be my pleasure, Amelia Ann."

And it was.

Eleven

Tyler drove up to the Beauchamp house in the old blue Chrysler and parked, breathing a small sigh of relief that he'd made it all the way back to Tulip without something falling off the ancient car, or it quitting on him.

He was anxious to see Amelia. Her unexpected arrival at his house had unleashed the passion between them. Just thinking about the sensuous way in which she'd returned his love made him sweat. He wiped his hands on his blue jeans as he got out of the Chrysler, trying to concentrate on other things. Wilhemina would have a stroke if he walked in the house with his libido this primed. It was going to be hell getting on the good side of that well-aged woman as it was, but he'd do it or die trying. Amelia and her aunts came packaged as a set of three.

As he walked up the steps then knocked, a flurry of footsteps inside the house made him chuckle. He could just imagine Wilhemina ordering the pillows to be fluffed and the magazines put back in order. And if he knew Rosemary, she was fussing with her hair and straightening her belt. But he didn't care, the woman he'd come to see was Amelia. He waited in anticipation, wondering which personality would greet him, Amelia of the staid propriety, or the Amber of his dreams?

Amelia hovered at the windows watching for Tyler's arrival. She knew Aunt Witty was upset about her interest in him, but she didn't know how to assure her that loving Tyler didn't mean she no longer loved her, too.

The night they'd made love had shifted their relationship onto a higher plane. She'd never known it could be possible to fall in love and have a nervous breakdown at the same time. If she didn't tell him soon about her deceit, she was going to lose what was left of her mind.

And then he drove up and her heart fell at her feet as she watched him walking toward the door. Oh God, she prayed. Don't let me lose this man.

A knock sounded throughout the house.

Rosemary jumped to her feet, patting at her hair and fussing with her collar as her cheeks turned a delicate shade of pink. "He's here!"

Amelia smiled. If she didn't know better, she'd think Rosemary was the one with a beau.

"I'll get it," Amelia said, and bolted for the door, knowing that if Aunt Rosie answered, she'd never get Tyler to herself. She hadn't seen him since their night together and leaving him later had been the hardest thing she'd ever had to do. She'd come home to a lonely bed and hadn't slept two good hours since. All she could remember was what it felt like to lose one's sense of self in a strong man's arms.

Wilhemina glared as Amelia raced toward the door. She heartily resented the fact that both Rosemary and Amelia had consorted with the enemy. It made her feel isolated and abandoned by the two she loved the most. How could they place so much importance on a *man's* appearance into their lives? Didn't they know that men weren't to be trusted?

Just as he was about to knock again, Amelia opened the door.

For a moment, she let her eyes feast on his wicked, knowing smile, his broad shoulders and those long legs. She shuddered slightly, remembering how strong they felt as he'd wrapped them around her body. Instead of throwing herself in his arms, she had to settle for the chaste kiss he gave her.

"Hello, Tyler. I'm glad you're here. Did you have any trouble with the Chrysler?"

Breath caught in the back of his throat as he looked at her and remembered, then he whispered for her ears only. "I'm glad I'm here, too." Then he spoke a little louder. "I didn't have a bit of trouble. The car seems to be running normally."

Rosemary perked up. The car was back! "That's good news," she chirped, and peered past the couple to the old blue car parked beside Amelia's new red one.

Tyler caught the gleam in Rosemary's eye and realized it was time to reveal his idea. He squeezed Amelia's hand and then greeted Wilhemina.

"Miss Wilhemina, I hope you're healing just fine."

She sniffed. If only he would show some boorish behavior, it would be easier to hate this man. "Thank you, Tyler. I suppose that I am."

He smiled. "That's good, because I have a proposition that might be of some interest to you."

Wilhemina pursed her lips, then fussed with her skirt tail, making certain that her wrapped ankle didn't show. It wasn't seemly.

"May I," he asked, waiting for permission from Wilhemina to sit beside her.

She sighed and nodded.

"Now that Amelia has her new car, I wondered if you ladies were considering putting the Chrysler up for sale.

What with the increase in traffic from the new highway leading into Savannah and the faster speed limits, I thought you and Miss Rosemary might not be so interested in getting behind the wheel anymore.''

Amelia clutched her hands behind her back, resisting the urge to throw them around Tyler's neck, instead. That was the most dear and diplomatic out she'd ever heard a person give another. Wilhemina and Rosemary had just been handed a much-needed excuse. Now they wouldn't have to admit they could no longer handle a car. All they had to do was agree with what he'd said. She held her breath, praying that Aunt Witty wouldn't balk.

Wilhemina's chin tilted angrily. She knew what he was getting at and certainly didn't like to be reminded of her age. But she also knew that when Rosemary had absconded with the Chrysler the other day, it was divine intervention alone that had kept her safe. That and the fact that Tyler Savage had driven her home. She disliked the notion of being indebted to a man for her sister's welfare. It made her next comment churlish.

''If we sell our car, how do you expect us to get around? Thanks to you, it's quite obvious that Amelia won't be around forever.''

The moment she spoke, she regretted what she'd said. The look of guilt on Amelia's face made her sick, but it was too late to take it back.

Rosemary gasped. It was the first time in her entire life she could ever remember Wilhemina being selfish.

''Willy! The very idea! Amelia has a right to her own life. She's under no obligation to wet-nurse us and you know it. I'm ashamed of you.''

Tyler's eyes narrowed as his thoughts scrambled for order. He knew what Wilhemina was up to. This only proved his theory that guilt had played a big part in Amelia's deceit. She was loaded with all kinds of hang-ups that these two elderly women had unwittingly built into her system.

If she'd had any sort of normal life, she would never have considered hiding her identity to obtain a second job.

Tyler slipped his hand over Wilhemina's and gently dropped the keys into her palm.

"You're the best judge for what's safe and proper, Miss Wilhemina," he said quietly. "But you should know something now. When I asked your permission to court Amelia, I had no intention of taking her away from you. On the contrary. I fully expected that if I was ever so lucky as to have Amelia for my wife, that you and your sister were part of the package. I was sort of counting on getting three women for the price of one."

And when he gave her a teasing wink, she turned red from the neck up.

Amelia blinked back tears. It was the single most endearing thing a man had ever said about her. She walked up behind him and slipped her hand on his shoulder, squeezing gently to remind him of her presence.

Wilhemina was trapped now and she knew it. "I'll have to think about selling the car. I don't suppose we'd get anything out of it. It's quite old."

"You might be surprised," he said. "If you're interested, let me know. I have a friend in Atlanta who restores old cars. He'd probably pay a premium for one in such good condition."

Wilhemina was intrigued in spite of herself. She had no intention of ever driving the car again, and if it was gone, Rosemary would have no opportunity.

"Really? Well then, I suppose you may give him our number. If I think it's fair, I might be interested."

"Yes, ma'am," Tyler said, trying not to grin. "If he calls, don't take less than five thousand dollars. He'll pay it if you remain firm."

Wilhemina's mouth dropped. "That's more than it cost new."

"Yes ma'am," he said, and then smiled at her. "But

sometimes things with 'character' are worth keeping—just like people.''

"We could buy that new dishwasher," Rosemary cried. "I'd love to have a dishwasher. You know how soap makes my hands burn. I have such delicate skin."

Wilhemina glared. "There is not one delicate thing about you, Rosemary. Lazy, maybe, but definitely not delicate."

"I'm not lazy," Rosemary argued. "I simply chose to live at a more 'leisurely' pace than you, dear. You should try it sometime. It's quite good for the digestion."

Amelia interrupted before their fuss escalated and Aunt Rosie got into colorful descriptions of digestion.

"You two talk it out," she said. "I'm going to run Tyler home. We've imposed on his time enough for one day."

"Oh no," he said, knowing full well how Amelia was going to take what he said. "You can impose on me any time you wish. I'm all yours."

Amelia tried not to blush. She knew darn good and well how much of him there was to take. Just thinking about it made her weak at the knees.

"And that reminds me, Amelia," Tyler continued, "I don't know what you have planned for today, but I have several errands to do in town and if we do them before you take me home, it might make you late getting home. If that's a problem, why don't you take me to the farm and I'll get my own truck. I can always come back in and…"

"Don't be silly. You went out of your way to return our property. The least I can do is return the favor." She picked up her purse. "Are you ready?"

He smiled slowly. "Yes, Amelia. I believe I am."

She looked everywhere and at everything but him as they walked out the door. The devil. He was flirting with her in the most devious manner. Everything he said had a sexual connotation that, thank God, only *she* understood.

It did nothing to embarrass her aunts and did everything to undermine her willpower.

"Where do you need to go first?" she asked, as Tyler crawled into the seat beside her.

"To bed with you."

Amelia stared. He wasn't kidding. The look in his eyes would have melted train tracks.

Her voice was breathless and more than slightly interested. "You don't have any errands?"

"No, darlin', I really don't. What I said was a lie. I wanted to take you home and make love to you. Somehow I didn't think your aunts would be interested in that particular fact."

"Oh, God," she moaned, and slammed the car into gear.

Tyler grinned. "No use talkin' to Him, He's on my side. Want me to drive?"

She spun out, leaving a flurry of new-mown grass and leaves in the air behind her as she headed for Main Street.

A trail of clothing began just inside Tyler's front door and continued all the way down the hall, ending at the foot of his bed. It was an incriminating trail of lust.

Tyler lay on his side with his head propped in one hand while his other hand traced the curves of Amelia's lush body. He had to admit that it was truly shameless the way he kept coercing her into his bed, but he'd do it again in a heartbeat just to hold her in his arms.

"Amelia…?"

She closed her eyes and moaned when his fingers began to circle. "What?"

He leaned over and kissed the tip of one breast. "You have the most glorious hair. Why don't you wear it down more often? Every time I see it wadded up in that tight knot on top of your head I have the most awful urge to take *it* down and your clothes off. Do you know what thoughts like that do to a man in public?"

She gasped as his hand slid up her stomach and came to rest above her rib cage. "I'm beginning to understand."

"I hope you do." He lifted himself up, then across her, pinning her to the bed. Moving in a slow, almost undetectable motion, he watched with delight at the way her pupils dilated with renewed passion. "You have the most beautiful eyes. I don't think I ever knew anyone with eyes just that color."

Amelia froze. Yes, you did. Have you forgotten how long you haunted a nightclub to persuade me...I mean Amber...to go out with you?

Instead of answering her, he began to rock himself against her. Just a little. Not too fast. And she forgot poor Amber who'd been dumped.

Tyler buttoned the last button on her dress and then teasingly held her hairpins behind his back, knowing full well she couldn't go home looking as if she'd just been taken to bed.

She laughed, grabbing toward his hands to retrieve the pins. "Please, Tyler, you know I can't go home looking like this. Aunt Witty would have a stroke and Aunt Rosie would ask me if the next time she could watch. I have a difficult enough time living in both worlds."

He paused. He'd never considered all of this from her point of view. It made everything she'd done suddenly seem plausible...even rational. He handed her the pins.

"What's going to happen to us if your Aunt Witty won't accept me? Who loses? Me...or the aunts?"

Tears welled. She ducked her head and buried her face against his chest.

"I don't want to have to choose. Why must I choose, Tyler? Why can't I have both?"

He wrapped his arms around her shaking shoulders. "Oh, darlin', I didn't mean *I* wanted you to choose. I'd take all three of you in a minute. You just say the word and I'll move every one of you out here if that's what it takes to get you in my life. And I'd never regret or resent it a bit.''

Amelia sighed. There were still so many problems she needed to resolve before she could even consider happy ever afters with Tyler. There were too many yesterdays between them.

She sighed and stepped back. "I know you think that, but they're quite a pair. You don't really know what you're asking for.'' Then she shrugged. "Besides, the point is moot. They wouldn't leave their home and I can't leave them helpless. I know they aren't now, but someday soon they will be. It's inevitable.''

"Then we'd deal with that when the time came. Don't borrow trouble, honey. If we take it one day at a time and share our feelings with each other, there won't be any hard feelings—or secrets between us.''

It was the mention of "sharing" followed by "secrets" that made her sick. They were in love, had made love, and she had yet to confess her own secret. How was Tyler going to react when she finally told him? Oh God, how has my life gotten into such a mess?

She kissed the edge of his lower lip and then glanced out the window. "It's nearly dark. I guess I'd better go. I don't want them to worry.''

As they walked outside to her car, he held her hand just that little bit tighter. Letting her go was the hardest thing he ever had to do, but he'd seen the hesitation in her eyes. He'd given her several openings to bring up her past and each time he'd seen panic flare and then watched as she let the moment pass. He sighed. One day she'd get up the courage, and when she did, he had something he wanted to say to her, too.

"I love you, Amelia.''

She grinned and threw her arms around his neck, then batted her eyes, pretending to simper like an old-fashioned, southern belle. "Oh, Tyler, you say the nicest things.''

He laughed aloud. She was such an enchanting mix of

stiff-backed librarian and sexy tease. Then to his delight, she pressed a swift kiss against his earlobe and then whispered softly.

"I love you, too, Tyler Dean."

It was several long moments later before he even knew she was gone. He'd been too lost in the wonder of hearing her say those words for the first time.

But when he walked back inside the house, he began to smile. There, hanging on the pink lamp shade his mother had purchased at Delia Mae Birney's Going Out of Business sale, was Amelia's bra.

His grin broadened as he pulled it down from the shade, and wrapped the bits of elastic and lace around his fingers. It was a good thing she was wearing a dress that didn't cling because Miss Wilhemina just might send the sheriff and his dogs out looking for him.

"Well, hell," he reminded himself, as he stuffed it in his bureau drawer. "She's worth at least a tar and feathering...if not a hanging, anyday."

Wilhemina stood in the doorway of the washroom with an armful of lingerie in her hands. "Rosemary, I must have dropped some of Amelia's undergarments. Would you please go upstairs and check the hamper?"

"How do you know you dropped something if you can't see it?"

She sighed with aggravated impatience. "Because I counted. I have six pair of nylon briefs and only five foundation garments. Therefore...I must have dropped one."

Rosemary stared. "You mean you count our panties?"

Wilhemina had the grace to flush. "Not exactly...but it seems only sensible to make certain that I have all the wash before I start the machine."

Rosemary was appalled that even at their ages, she was learning of still another of her sister's foibles.

"And why you insist on calling a brassiere a foundation garment is beyond me, Sister. The fashionable thing is to call them 'bras.' I have even heard them called holsters, but I think that's a bit..."

Wilhemina gasped. "My stars! Just go upstairs and see if I dropped one, will you? I still have trouble negotiating those stairs. Too many trips up and down makes my ankle swell."

Rosemary sighed. "Oh, all right, but I think you're making a fuss over nothing. If you missed it this time, you can always wash it later."

Wilhemina glared.

Rosemary hastened to do her sister's bidding. It was a habit too old to break.

But to Rosemary's dismay, there were no wispy undergarments in the hallway, nor in the hamper inside Amelia's room and knowing Willy, she couldn't go back without it. She sat on the side of the bed, puzzling the whereabouts of the missing bra when Amelia came into the room.

"Why, hello dear," Rosemary said, as a smile of welcome beamed across her face. "You're just in time. Willy sent me up here to find the rest of your laundry."

The smile on Amelia's face stopped just short of wide. She had a horrifying suspicion of what Aunt Rosie was going to say next. "Laundry?"

Rosemary giggled girlishly. "Actually it's just one of your bras. Did you know that Willy counts panties? I swear, that woman is losing her marbles, don't you know."

"Panties?"

Amelia could definitely remember coming home wearing panties, but she'd missed the bra almost the moment she'd started up the stairs to her room. The gentle and unmistakable sway of unfettered breasts beneath her dress had been all the reminder she needed to remember that she'd left more than her heart with Tyler.

Rosemary continued as if Amelia had never answered. "Actually, she counts everything, and she swears that she dropped one of your bras when she started the wash. Do you know where it might be?''

Amelia rolled her eyes. She knew very well where it was. However, she seriously doubted that Aunt Witty would want to know.

"I'll look," she said. "Why don't you go on back to your television program? I'm sure it's around somewhere."

Rosemary beamed again. "Thank you, dear. You're so thoughtful."

When Rosemary was gone, Amelia dashed to her dresser and pulled out a clean brasserie, rumpling it a bit before running into the bathroom to spray it with deodorant. She took the stairs back down two at a time.

"Here it is, Aunt Witty," she said, and dangled the bra over the washer before stuffing it in with the rest of the lingerie.

Wilhemina nodded, satisfied that she'd been justified in her worry.

Amelia watched the bra disappear beneath the soap and water as it mixed with the rest of her wash. If only my problems could be washed away as easily as this. I've got to find a way to tell Tyler the truth, and I've got to do it soon.

Twelve

Wilhemina stood on the front porch, watching the man from Atlanta driving away with the Chrysler.

Rosemary sniffed and then blew her nose briskly. "I truly loved that car,"

"Yes, I know, Sister, but I think this is compensation enough for the vehicle." She waved the five thousand dollar cashier's check beneath Rosemary's nose and then folded it and slipped it into her pocket.

Rosemary beamed. "And we'd have none of this if it weren't for Tyler."

Wilhemina's smile slipped. She hated to admit it but her sister was right. She turned, staring at the new window he'd helped replace after the storm, and the stump from the missing tree by the driveway that he'd helped clear away, not to mention the new roof that the insurance company had already completed.

And all this had happened while she had lain helpless in a Savannah hospital. And then there were the changes she kept seeing in Amelia. It wasn't only her style of dress, her behavior had definitely taken a turn, too. In her day, openly hugging or kissing a suitor hadn't been done.

Still, she had to admit that Tyler was nothing if not proper. But it still rankled that after all she'd done to insure Amelia's well-being and behavior, it had only taken one man to undo everything she'd tried to accomplish.

And then to her dismay, the object of her discontent came down the street and parked in their driveway. Rosemary ran to meet him, flitting through the grass like a schoolgirl.

"Why, Tyler! If you'd only been a few minutes sooner, you could have spoken to your friend from Atlanta," Rosemary said, and beamed as Tyler bent down and kissed her cheek.

"Sold the car, did you?" he asked, and tried not to smile at the wistful expression in Rosemary's eyes. Remembering her trip to his farm still gave him the shudders. Selling it had happened none too soon.

Wilhemina bristled as she watched her sister accept his familiarity. He'd better not try anything so forward on her! She wasn't the kissing type.

Tyler eyed the elder sister as he stepped onto the porch, figuring that he'd given her enough time to adjust to the fact that he was on their property.

"Miss Wilhemina,"

"Amelia's not here," she said shortly.

"Yes, ma'am. I didn't come to see her. I came to see you."

She flushed. She hated confrontations. "I suppose since you're here you may as well come in," she said grudgingly.

She had no intention of having a disagreement in plain sight of Effie. She no longer came to their house everyday, but she'd taken it upon herself to drop in way too often for Wilhemina's peace of mind.

"If you don't mind, ma'am, I'd rather sit out on your

front porch. As you can see I'm not clean enough to sit on any of your fine furniture. I came straight from the field to pick up a repair part. I've been wanting to talk to you when we wouldn't be interrupted and this seemed as good a time as any.''

Rosemary clapped her hands. "I'll get us something cold to drink. You and Willy sit right down. It won't take me a minute," she said, and bustled into the house. Her tennis shoes made a squeak-squeak noise on the shiny hardwood floor as she hurried down the hallway and into the kitchen.

Wilhemina slipped into one of the pair of wicker chairs on the veranda and then frowned as Tyler chose the porch swing instead. It was strange how alike men were. Poppa had always refused to sit in wicker, saying it wasn't manly. Now, here was this man, two generations removed, doing the same odd thing.

There was no point in wasting breath on small talk. It was obvious that he didn't like her. Men never had. And that was all right, she thought, because she hadn't liked them, either. "So, what brings you here?"

"You," he said quietly.

His blue eyes pierced her conscience as she watched the lines tighten around his mouth, but she wouldn't give an inch and waited for him to continue.

Tyler settled into the swing and stretched his arms along the back, then pushed himself off with one booted toe and cocked his head, allowing the gentle rocking motion to calm the worry that had accompanied him to town.

"You know that you and Miss Rosemary are the two single most important people in Amelia's life. Personally, I think you're all genuinely lucky. It's rare that three women can live in a house together and remain friends as well as family.''

Wilhemina blinked. It was an observation she'd never considered. Grudgingly, she had to admit he might be right.

"I suppose, but Rosemary and I don't agree on much of anything."

He smiled. "That may be so, ma'am. But I'd warrant that it does nothing to diminish the love you feel for each other…am I right?"

She looked away. Focusing on the manicured lawns and the perfectly positioned flower beds, she thought over what he was saying and finally nodded.

"So, where is this conversation leading, Tyler Dean, and don't think I don't know you want to take Amelia away from us."

The quiver in her voice made him sad. He could see how deeply she was fighting her feelings. He also knew that she'd die before she cried in front of him.

He stopped the motion of the swing and leaned forward, taking her shaky hands gently within his grasp. "No, dear. I don't want to take her away from you. I want you to share her with me."

Forty years of suppressed tears shot forth. She blinked rapidly and tried to pull away from his grip. Instead, he gently placed a clean and folded handkerchief into her hands and then turned away, giving her time to compose herself.

"Thank you," she said, and blotted her eyes, resisting the urge to blow her nose. It wouldn't be seemly to hand a handkerchief back in that condition, so she settled for a subdued sniff instead. His words had touched her deeply. It was time for her to face the facts.

In her heart, she knew that despite his "bad boy" reputation, this man had done nothing but stand up for Amelia since he'd entered their lives. She also knew without a doubt that his appearance on their doorstep in the middle of the worst of the gossip had been an instant muzzle on the town of Tulip. She also knew that he was well-to-do and hard-working, and although he *was* a man, was a well-respected member of Tulip's society. What he'd done for them after the storm was no small gesture, either. With a defeated sigh, she leaned back in the wicker chair and stared across their lawn.

Tyler watched her from the corner of his eye. He could see her emotions were in upheaval. Her sense of fair play was playing hell with her opinion of the male species. That much was obvious. And the tears in her eyes told him, as nothing else could, that she truly loved Amelia and wanted the best for her. It was the first sign Tyler'd had that gave him hope.

"So, what do you think?" he asked, and held his breath, praying that what she said would be the right answer. It was moments before she spoke.

She handed his handkerchief back with an abrupt thrust of her hand, and then settled herself primly into the chair.

"I think that it doesn't much matter what I say. I think she's going to do what she pleases." She glared at him, daring him to contradict.

It wasn't what he wanted to hear. But it wasn't a no.

"Then I don't think you know Amelia as well as you think you do," Tyler said. "If you object, she'll bow to your wishes. She won't walk out on you and Rosemary, even if it means she spends the rest of her life alone."

Wilhemina was aghast. She'd been so entrenched in the present, she'd not considered the future. And for Amelia, it would mean loneliness.

"Oh my...I didn't think of that." She looked away, unable to meet his gaze. "I suppose you think that I'm awfully selfish."

"No, ma'am, I don't."

He rose from the swing and started toward the front door. He could hear Rosemary coming back. Glasses clinked against one another as she struggled with her tray of refreshments. He walked past Wilhemina and then stopped and turned.

For one long moment, he stared at the stiff tilt of her neck and the small tight wad of gray hair on the top of her head. She would have hated to know how vulnerable she looked. He sighed and then smiled, and before she knew it, he had kissed her on the forehead.

"I don't think you're selfish. I think you're a lovin' woman, Wilhemina. Just let me in on a little of it. I won't ask for much…except maybe extras on your cookin'."

She was speechless and more than a little bit touched by what he'd said and done.

And then Tyler opened the door and relieved Rosemary of her loaded tray before it went flying, and her with it. He set the tray onto the table between the wicker chairs and then seated Rosemary beside her sister. "This looks fine, Miss Rosemary. Did you make these cookies?"

She giggled and patted her hair. "Mercy no! And you'd better be glad. I can't cook worth a darn."

Wilhemina rolled her eyes. "Rosemary, don't blaspheme!"

"Darn isn't a bad word," Rosemary insisted, as she served lemonade and cookies to Tyler and then to her sister. "It's what you do to mend socks." Her eyes twinkled as Tyler winked at her.

He swallowed a laugh along with a huge bite of cookie. These two were priceless. And the best part was, he could see bits and pieces of Amelia in each of them.

"Whoever made these cookies did a bang-up job," he said, and willingly took a second helping that Rosemary offered.

Wilhemina tried not to preen, but in her world, praise was rare.

"Sister made them," Rosemary offered. "She can make just about anything."

The look that passed between Wilhemina and himself was slow in coming, but when it did, it was filled with acceptance and understanding. He cocked an eyebrow and grinned.

"If Amelia can cook half as well as you, I just might not starve after all."

Rosemary giggled and then gawked at the look on her sister's face. Wilhemina was smiling!

Amelia tried not to lean on the hot leather car seats as she swiftly rolled down her window. There was no need even turning on the air conditioner. She'd be home before it had a chance to get cool.

Her car started with a gentle purr and she smiled to herself as she headed for home. At least something she owned was in perfect working order. But as she turned the corner toward home and saw a red-and-white pickup sitting in her driveway, she became certain that what was left of the order in her life was about to come to an end.

The sight of Tyler having cookies and lemonade with the aunts left her speechless. Fear spiked. What had they been discussing?

Oh Lord, I never did tell them that Tyler doesn't know about my life as Amber. And I didn't tell them not to tell. I knew I shouldn't have put this off. She got out of the car with trepidation, her voice just the least bit hesitant.

"Hello, everyone."

Tyler was at her side in an instant. With one hand beneath her elbow to steady her, he quickly relieved her of her briefcase and purse and had her sitting beside him in the swing sipping lemonade before she had time to panic. She glanced at him and then at Aunt Witty and caught a look that passed between them. Had they been arguing? Dear God, please, not that!

"My," she said brightly, "this is an unexpected pleasure. I didn't know you were coming to town, Tyler."

He grinned. "It wasn't planned, but when I drove by, I couldn't seem to pass without stopping. And then I was offered some of the best cookies in town. After that..." He shrugged and took another cookie from the plate.

Amelia gawked as Aunt Witty actually preened beneath the compliment. What in heaven's name has happened? She stared around in amazement.

I know! I'm dreaming. Any minute I'll wake up and have to shower and dress and go to work. This just isn't happening because I saw Aunt Witty grin.

Tyler knew Amelia was nervous. He could see her shaking, and her smile was too fixed, her eyes were too bright. She looked to be close to hysterics or tears, and he was in no mood for either.

"It's okay, darlin'," he said softly, and kissed the corner of her temple. "We've just been talkin'."

It was subdued and subtle, but it was as public as kisses get. Rosemary clapped her hands. "When's the wedding?"

Wilhemina frowned. "Rosemary, your manners are lacking. What will Tyler think of us?"

Amelia nearly fell out of the swing. "Aunt Rosie! What ever made you say something like that?"

Her heart gave a thud! This would fix it! Tyler'd be gone in a flash. Nothing like being backed into a corner to send a man packing.

But Tyler just laughed. Not a little, and not quietly. He leaned his head back and laughed until he was choking for air. He laughed until tears hung at the corners of his eyes. More than once he tried to stop, but every time he looked at the shock on Amelia's face and the overdone innocence on Rosemary's, it came back in full force.

Rosemary was a case and there was no mistaking it, but to make matters worse, he suspected she wasn't nearly as flighty as she pretended. A grin was lingering on his face just as Amelia bolted for the house.

"Oh my!" Rosemary gasped, and pressed a hand to her bosom. "I didn't mean to offend. Maybe I'd better…"

"No, ma'am," Tyler said, choking back the last of his laughter. "Let me."

He caught her just before she ran up the stairs.

"Amelia, darlin', don't be upset."

She couldn't look him in the face.

He sighed. Nothing like back to square one. "She only beat me to the punch, you know," he said softly.

Amelia jerked, but he refused to let her move. Humiliation swamped her. Now Tyler was stuck with either backing out on their relationship, or being forced into making a decision for which he might not be ready. She could cheerfully strangle Aunt Rosie.

His eyes narrowed thoughtfully. "Okay, fine. I'll give you two hours to pull yourself together, Amelia Ann, and then I'm coming back and we're going out to dinner. After that, we're going to my place. Besides other things, we're going to talk, and I don't want to hear any arguments, okay?"

She sighed in defeat and then looked up. "Okay," she said, but he hadn't even waited for her answer. He was already walking out the door.

Dinner had been a strained affair.

Amelia couldn't say exactly what she'd eaten. And she had no idea what they'd talked about, although she vaguely remembered trying to keep a halfhearted conversation alive. It was when they headed for the farm that she started to worry. There were so many things she needed to say and she had not the first instinct as to how to start.

Tyler hit a bump in the road and grabbed her leg, absently steadying her as he guided his vehicle around an even larger dip as he muttered. "Darn roadbed. They need to grade these roads at least more than once every six months. The ruts get worse every time it rains...and it's been doing enough of that lately."

Amelia nodded. Rough roads and weather were not what was worrying her. The driveway leading to Tyler's home appeared in the distance. She held her breath, expecting he'd been practicing a long-winded excuse for why they shouldn't see each other anymore.

Tears filled her eyes. She ducked her head and stared at her lap, trying desperately not to cry. She would survive. This had happened to her before. She'd lived through it then, she'd live through it now.

And then she looked up at the strong profile of Tyler's face highlighted by the lights from the dashboard and knew there was no way she'd ever get over losing this man. It would be like losing a part of herself.

"God help me," she muttered, and rubbed her finger up and down the bridge of her nose, praying she'd hadn't been wrong about Tyler's intentions. He'd sworn he loved her. She just hoped it was enough to include all of the Beauchamp women. Including Amber.

Tyler pulled up, then parked and killed the engine. "What did you say, darlin'?"

She shrugged. "Nothing, just talking to myself."

He leaned over and kissed her full on the mouth, lingering longer than necessary on her lower lip. "Come inside and talk to me instead," he whispered, and smiled as he watched her face light up.

But once inside, Amelia could hardly face him. They were alone in his house with this awful silence between them and her untold secret eating at her insides.

Where do I start? Admit to Tyler that I'm a fraud, or just let him off the hook and try not to die?

She took a deep breath and turned to face him, but he was closer than she'd expected. In fact, he was so close that when she turned, their lips grazed. She gasped with surprise and then went limp as Tyler took her in his arms and proceeded to explore what she'd unexpectedly offered.

"I have something of yours," he said, and gave her one last kiss. "Wait here."

When he came back, her eyes widened as he dropped her missing bra in her hands, then she groaned beneath her breath and stuffed it in her purse, embarrassed by its presence.

He laughed and swept her off her feet and into his arms. "Save room for the one you're wearing, cause it's comin' off, too."

She choked back a sob, willing to allow him whatever he wanted. It might be the last time in her life she ever knew such joy. She wanted to remember everything about this man for when she was old and alone. At least she'd have something besides regrets for company.

And then everything was forgotten as the business of coming out of their clothes and into his bed became too important to ignore. He turned her around and lifted her hair to unzip her dress, leaving tiny kisses down the path of skin the open zipper revealed. "I love you, Amelia...so much."

She shuddered as his hands slid beneath the silky fabric to cup the fullness of her breasts. She leaned back against him as the top of her dress fell to her waist. "I love you, too, Tyler. But I don't want you to feel pressured by what Aunt Rosie said."

"I'm sorry, darlin', but that's impossible. If I feel any more pressure, I'm likely to explode," and then he moved himself against her hips to emphasize his point.

She sighed and then shuddered as his hands slid down and her dress slid off. Moments later they were side by side on his bed, lost in the overwhelming need to belong to each other.

Her hands sought him out, searching and then moving across his body in a way that made sanity impossible. He rolled over and moved above her, then nearly passed out from the feelings she sent rocketing through his body as her hands slipped lower, encircling him, stroking him.

Tears filled her eyes as she watched the joy on his face. It was something she'd never forget. That she was capable of giving him so much pleasure was almost too much to believe.

Her arms encircled his neck. "Love me," she whispered.

"Always," he promised, and then lost himself in her heat. A growl of satisfaction came up his throat as he lowered his head and captured her lips with his own. When she arched to meet his entry, there was no more thought, only feeling.

Joy became pleasure, pleasure became need. And finally the need became an enduring pain as Amelia cried for release.

Tyler was showing her in the only way he knew how that she was everything to him. And then passion superseded sanity as he lost himself in his sweet woman's arms.

Afterglow only lasts so long. And then, as always, comes reality. Amelia moaned and turned her face into the curve of his neck as he held her fast. She'd put this off too long, but hoped the old saying "better late than never" would hold true. She simply could not lose this man and his love because of a lie. She took a deep breath and said a quick, silent prayer.

"Tyler?"

He shifted her against his chest and slid his hands up her back, tunneling through the rich tangle he'd made of her hair and tried not to smile. She was finally going to tell him, he could feel it!

Letting his fingers drift back down her waist and then lower, lingering on the curve of her hips with loving determination, he murmured, "What, darlin'?"

Amelia gritted her teeth. "I can't think when you do that," she said.

He grinned. "Thank God. You don't want me to think I'm losing my touch, do you?"

She crawled to a sitting position and punched him on the arm. "You are too cocky for your own good."

Amelia wasn't in the habit of parading naked in front of anybody, let alone a man, and from this position it was just the least bit embarrassing. She grabbed at a sheet, pulling it across her front and trying not to blush at the fact that Tyler refused to cover himself. When he ignored her distress, she glared at his wicked, knowing grin.

"As I was saying," she began again, and frowned when he began pulling at the sheet with his toes, trying to unveil her.

When she glared again, he paused, all innocence. "I'm listening."

"There's something I've been wanting to say to you for some time now."

"Me too, darlin'," Tyler interrupted. "I've been wondering all this time when I could ask you to marry me. I think now's as good a time as any. After all, I've more or less got you right where I want you."

"Oh...my! I'd love...I'd be most..." Then she gulped and froze. In the time it took to blink, she went from pale to pink and back again. The sheet fell from her fingers and down into a white wad in her lap. While he watched in dismay, she stuttered once and then started to cry.

Amelia was heartsick. Now he'd done it! It was what she'd wanted to hear ever since she'd first seen Tyler Savage on the streets of Tulip, and he'd gone and asked her before she could confess. What was going to happen now? She still had to say it, but it was going to kill her if he got so angry he took everything back.

He sat up and took her into his arms, then pulled her into his lap and rocked her, wadded up sheet and all. "Don't, Amelia. Please don't cry! My God, darlin', it wasn't supposed to make you sad. I just want to spend the rest of my life with you. Is that so bad?"

Tears fell faster. A few sobs even bubbled up and entered the scene on a hiccup.

"You don't understand..."

He sighed. It was time to let her off the hook before he got himself in trouble, too, although he'd figured it had been her secret to tell, not his to reveal. Obviously it was going to be more than she could manage with dignity. And when a man loves a woman, he never wants her stripped of her dignity. Maybe all her clothes...but never her dignity.

He cupped her face in his hands and swiped at the flow of tears with his thumbs as he leaned forward and tasted them on her lips. "I understand a whole lot more than you think, and I still want you to marry me...but on one condition.''

Oh God! Here it comes. I should have known there'd be a catch in this. If he's going to make me tell Aunt Rosie and Aunt Witty that I can't...

He grinned wickedly, reminding Amelia of Effie Dettenberg's warnings of Savage men and their savage instincts. ''And the condition is, that you be Amelia all day every day for the rest of our lives...but you have to be Amber by night!''

Her mouth dropped as she took a slow shuddering breath. He knew! The sorry sucker knew!

Indignation was forming behind those blue-green eyes when Tyler lay her down and then pinned her to the bed with more than gentle persuasion.

''Well,'' he asked, as he slid between her legs, ''Will you?''

''Lord have mercy,'' Amelia gasped, and closed her eyes as a slow smile of delight spread across her face. ''How could a woman ever tell you no?''

Epilogue

Wilhemina wadded the handkerchief she was holding and blinked rapidly, trying very hard not to cry in front of the congregation. She consoled herself with the fact that even if she did, it would probably be forgiven. After all, one was supposed to cry at weddings.

Rosemary sniffled between smiles of satisfaction as she watched the look on Tyler's face turn to one of pure joy. The minister raised his hands, indicating that the congregation stand. Rosemary clapped her hands together in childlike delight. Amelia must be coming!

Raelene Stringer was in her glory. Serving as Amelia's maid of honor was more than an honor. Making her a part of the wedding had also made Raelene a part of polite society. She stifled a grin at the looks of amazement on the congregation, and then caught her breath when she looked up the aisle.

Effie Dettenberg's smile froze in place as Rosemary looked her way. It wasn't anything obvious, but there was something about the set of her mouth that reminded Effie of their deal, so she pursed her lips and straightened her belt. With gusto, she began hammering the chords of the wedding march. As church organist, it was her job to play.

Amelia's heart was full. Her family was intact and, had in fact, grown by one more—the man who was waiting for her at the end of the aisle. A discreet smile slid into place as she neared the altar, thinking about what she'd packed in her luggage for their honeymoon.

Thanks to Raelene, she had one shiny red spandex outfit, black bustle, black fishnet hose and all. When she came out of the bathroom tonight, Tyler was going to be in for a big surprise. He wanted Amber by night…he was going to get her.

Tyler caught his breath at her beauty, watching as she came closer and closer. With every step she took, his world wasn't narrowing, it was expanding. He knew for a fact he was acquiring the most desirable mix of femininity to ever come out of Tulip, Georgia.

And then she was at the altar, and they were holding hands. The minister began intoning in solemn voice the seriousness of the vows they were about to exchange while Tyler held his breath. She was so beautiful…almost untouchable in all this white lace and satin. His fingers shook as their hands touched. He looked up and then forgot what he was supposed to say next.

Amelia was smiling. Slowly. Seductively. Hidden to all but his eyes, the tiniest tip of her tongue slid across her lower lip. And then the most audacious thing happened. Amelia Ann Beauchamp, librarian of Tulip, Georgia, winked at her groom in the middle of the ceremony like a flirty little tart.

He choked on a laugh and then squeezed her hand tight. Something told him this marriage was going to be a wild ride through life. Personally, he could hardly wait.

*   *   *   *   *

Don't miss the latest miniseries from award-winning author Marie Ferrarella:

Meet...

Sherry Campbell—ambitious newswoman who makes headlines when a handsome billionaire arrives to sweep her off her feet...and shepherd her new son into the world!
A BILLIONAIRE AND A BABY, SE#1528,
available March 2003

Joanna Prescott—Nine months after her visit to the sperm bank, her old love rescues her from a burning house—then delivers her baby....
A BACHELOR AND A BABY, SD#1503,
available April 2003

Chris "C.J." Jones—FBI agent, expectant mother and always on the case. When the baby comes, will her irresistible partner be by her side?
THE BABY MISSION, IM#1220, available May 2003

Lori O'Neill—A forbidden attraction blows down this pregnant Lamaze teacher's tough-woman facade and makes her consider the love of a lifetime!
BEAUTY AND THE BABY, SR#1668,
available June 2003

The Mom Squad—these single mothers-to-be are ready for labor...and true love!

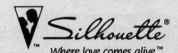

Where love comes alive™

COMING NEXT MONTH

#1501 TAMING THE BEASTLY MD—Elizabeth Bevarly
Dynasties: The Barones
When nurse Rita Barone needed a date for a party, she asked the very intriguing Dr. Matthew Grayson. Things heated up, and Rita wound up in Matthew's bed, where he introduced her to sensual delight. However, the next morning they vowed to forget their night of passion. But Rita couldn't forget. Could she convince the good doctor she needed his loving touch—*forever?*

#1502 INSTINCTIVE MALE—Cait London
Heartbreakers
Desperate for help, Ellie Lathrop turned to the one man who'd always gotten under her skin—enigmatic Mikhail Stepanov. Mikhail ignited Ellie's long-hidden desires, and soon she surrendered to their powerful attraction. But proud Mikhail wouldn't accept less than her whole heart, and Ellie didn't know if she could give him that.

#1503 A BACHELOR AND A BABY—Marie Ferrarella
The Mom Squad
Because of a misunderstanding, Rick Masters had lost Joanna Prescott, the love of his life. But eight years later, Rick drove past Joanna's house—just in time to save her from a fire and deliver her baby. The old chemistry was still there, and Rick fell head over heels for Joanna and her baby. But Joanna feared being hurt again; could Rick prove his love was rock solid?

#1504 TYCOON FOR AUCTION—Katherine Garbera
When Corrine Martin won sexy businessman Rand Pearson at a bachelor auction, she decided he would make the perfect corporate boyfriend. Their arrangement consisted of three dates. But Corrine found pleasure and comfort in Rand's embrace, and she found herself in unanticipated danger—of surrendering to love!

#1505 BILLIONAIRE BOSS—Meagan McKinney
Matched in Montana
He had hired her to be his assistant, but when wealthy Seth Morgan came face-to-face with beguiling beauty Kirsten Meadows, he knew he wanted to be more than just her boss. Soon he was fighting to persuade wary Kirsten to yield to him—one sizzling kiss at a time!

#1506 WARRIOR IN HER BED—Cathleen Galitz
Annie Wainwright had gone to Wyoming seeking healing, not romance. Then Johnny Lonebear stormed into her life, refusing to be ignored. Throwing caution to the wind, Annie embarked on a summer fling with Johnny that grew into something much deeper. But what would happen once Johnny learned she was carrying his child?

SDCNM0303